"Mankind has dire legends of hybrids produced by the cross-breeding of various species. Among these are the chimera, the griffin and the sphinx, to name but a few. It seems to me that these antique nightmares might have been a *memory of the future*—like Garcia's perception of my not-yet-committed crimes.

"The scientists of today will deny its existence even when my heraldic beasts are swarming into towns and cities. No reasonable man will believe in a creature the size of a wolf, as savage and cunning as a wolverine, as social, adaptable, and as great a breeder as a rat. A confirmed rationalist will deny credence to this indescribable and apocryphal beast even as it tears out his throat.

"And he will be almost right in his skepticism. Such a product of cross-hybridization was clearly impossible—until I produced it last year."

Just a tidbit from one of the fabulous tales that make up Robert Sheckley's latest collection of unique science fiction!

CAN YOU FEEL ANYTHING WHEN I DO THIS?

by
Robert Sheckley

DAW BOOKS, INC.
DONALD A. WOLLHEIM, PUBLISHER

1301 Avenue of the Americas
New York, N. Y.   10019

COPYRIGHT ©, 1961, 1968, 1969, 1970, 1971,
BY ROBERT SHECKLEY.

A DAW Book,
by arrangement with Doubleday & Co., Inc.

All Rights Reserved.

Cover art by Hans Arnold.

Ten of the stories included in this collection were originally published in magazines as follows:

"Can You Feel Anything When I Do This?", "Cordle to Onion to Carrot," "The Same to You Doubled," and "Pas de Trois of the Chef and the Waiter and the Customer" (this last story under the title of "Three Sinners in the Green Jade Moon") in *Playboy*; "The Petrified World" in *IF*; "The Cruel Equations" and "Tripout" in *BOAC*; "Starting from Scratch" and "Tailpipe to Disaster" in *The Magazine of Fantasy and Science Fiction;* and "Down the Digestive Tract and into the Cosmos with Mantra, Tantra, and Specklebang" (under the title of "Down the Digestive Tract") in *Galaxy*.

FIRST PRINTING, APRIL 1974

1 2 3 4 5 6 7 8 9

PRINTED IN U.S.A.

TABLE OF CONTENTS

Can You Feel Anything When I Do This?	7
Cordle to Onion to Carrot	19
The Petrified World	36
Game: First Schematic	46
Doctor Zombie and His Little Furry Friends	51
The Cruel Equations	63
The Same to You Doubled	79
Starting from Scratch	90
The Mnemone	95
Tripout	105
Notes on the Perception of Imaginary Differences	116
Down the Digestive Tract and into the Cosmos with Mantra, Tantra, and Specklebang	122
Pas de Trois of the Chef and the Waiter and the Customer	125
Aspects of Langranak	141
Plague Circuit	146
Tailpipe to Disaster	153

To Abby

CAN YOU FEEL ANYTHING WHEN I DO THIS?

It was a middle-class apartment in Forest Hills with all the standard stuff: slash-pine couch by Lady Yogina, strobe reading light over a big Uneasy Chair designed by Sri Somethingorother, bounce-sound projector playing *Blood-Stream Patterns* by Drs. Molidoff and Yuli. There was also the usual microbiotic-food console, set now at Fat Black Andy's Soul-Food Composition Number Three—hog's jowls and black-eyed peas. And there was a Murphy Bed of Nails, the Beautyrest Expert Ascetic model with 2000 chrome-plated self-sharpening number-four nails. In a sentence, the whole place was furnished in a pathetic attempt at last year's *moderne-spirituel* fashion.

Inside this apartment, all alone and aching of *anomie*, was a semi-young housewife, Melisande Durr, who had just stepped out of the voluptuarium, the largest room in the home, with its king-size commode and its sadly ironic bronze lingam and yoni on the wall.

She was a *pretty* girl, with really good legs, sweet hips, pretty stand-up breasts, long soft shiny hair, delicate little face. Nice, very nice. A girl that any man would like to lock onto. Once. Maybe even twice. But definitely not as a regular thing.

Why not? Well, to give you a recent example:

"Hey, Sandy, honey, was anything wrong?"

"No, Frank, it was marvelous; what made you think anything was wrong?"

"Well, I guess it was the way you were staring up with a funny look on your face, almost frowning. . . ."

"Was I really? Oh, yes, I remember; I was trying to decide whether to buy one of those cute trompe-l'oeil things that they just got in at Saks, to put on the ceiling."

"You were thinking about *that*? *Then*?"

"Oh, Frank, you mustn't worry, it was *great*, Frank, *you* were great, I loved it, and I really mean that."

Frank was Melisande's husband. He plays no part in this story and very little part in her life.

So there she was, standing in her OK apartment, all beautiful outside and unborn inside, a lovely potential who had never been potentiated, a genuine U.S. untouchable . . . when the doorbell rang.

Melisande looked startled, then uncertain. She waited. The doorbell rang again. She thought: *Someone must have the wrong apartment*.

Nevertheless, she walked over, set the Door-Gard Entrance Obliterator to demolish any rapist or burglar or wise guy who might try to push his way in, then opened the door a crack and asked, "Who is there, please?"

A man's voice replied, "Acme Delivery Service, got a mumble here for Missus Mumble-mumble."

"I can't understand, you'll have to speak up."

"Acme Delivery, got a mumble for mumble-mumble and I can't stand here all mumble."

"I cannot understand you!"

"I SAID I GOT A PACKAGE HERE FOR MISSUS MELISANDE DURR, DAMN IT!"

She opened the door all the way. Outside, there was a deliveryman with a big crate, almost as big as he was, say, five feet, nine inches tall. It had her name and address on it. She signed for it, as the deliveryman pushed it inside the door and left, still mumbling. Melisande stood in her living room and looked at the crate.

She thought: Who would send me a gift out of the blue for no reason at all? Not Frank, not Harry, not Aunt Emmie or Ellie, not Mom, not Dad (of course not, silly, he's five years dead, poor son of a bitch) or anyone I can think of. But maybe it's not a gift; it could be a mean hoax, or a bomb intended for somebody else and sent wrong (or meant for me and sent *right*) or just a simple mistake.

She read the various labels on the outside of the crate. The article had been sent from Stern's department store. Melisande bent down and pulled out the cotter pin (cracking the tip of a fingernail) that immobilized the Saftee-Lok, removed that and pushed the lever to OPEN.

The crate blossomed like a flower, opening into twelve equal segments, each of which began to fold back on itself.

"Wow," Melisande said.

The crate opened to its fullest extent and the folded segments curled inward and consumed themselves, leaving a double handful of cold fine gray ash.

"They still haven't licked that ash problem," Melisande muttered. "However."

She looked with curiosity at the object that had resided within the crate. At first glance, it was a cylinder of metal painted orange and red. A machine? Yes, definitely a machine; air vents in the base for its motor, four rubber-clad wheels, and various attachments—longitudinal extensors, prehensile extractors, all sorts of things. And there were connecting points to allow a variety of mixed-function operations, and a standard house-type plug at the end of a springloaded reel-fed power line, with a plaque beneath it that read: PLUG INTO ANY 110–115-VOLT WALL OUTLET.

Melisande's face tightened in anger. "It's a goddamned *vacuum cleaner!* For God's sake, I've already *got* a vacuum cleaner. Who in the hell would send me another?"

She paced up and down the room, bright legs flashing, tension evident in her heart-shaped face. "I mean," she said, "I was expecting that after all my *expecting*, I'd get something pretty and nice, or at least *fun*, maybe even interesting. Like—oh God I don't even know like what unless maybe an orange-and-red pinball machine, a big one, big enough so I could get inside all curled up and someone would start the game and I'd go bumping along all the bumpers while the lights flashed and bells rang and I'd bump a thousand goddamned bumpers and when I finally rolled down to the end I'd God yes that pinball machine would register a TOP MILLION MILLION and that's what I'd really like!"

So—the entire unspeakable fantasy was out in the open at last. And how bleak and remote it felt, yet still shameful and desirable.

"But anyhow," she said, canceling the previous image and folding, spindling and mutilating it for good measure, "anyhow, what I get is a lousy goddamned vacuum cleaner when I already have one less than three years old so who needs this one and who sent me the damned thing anyway and why?"

She looked to see if there was a card. No card. Not a clue. And then she thought, Sandy, you are really a goop! Of course, there's no card; the machine has doubtless been programmed to recite some message or other.

She was interested now, in a mild, something-to-do kind of way. She unreeled the power line and plugged it into a wall outlet.

Click! A green light flashed on, a blue light glittered ALL SYSTEMS GO, a motor purred, hidden servos made tapping noises; and then the mechanopathic regulator registered BALANCE and a gentle pink light beamed a steady ALL MODES READY.

"All right," Melisande said. "Who sent you?"

Snap crackle pop. Experimental rumble from the thoracic voice box. Then the voice: "I am Rom, number 121376 of GE's new Q-series Home-rizers. The following is a paid commercial announcement: Ahem, General Electric is proud to present the latest and most triumphant development of our Total Finger-Tip Control of Every Aspect of the Home for Better Living concept. I, Rom, am the latest and finest model in the GE Omnicleaner series. I am the Home-rizer Extraordinary, factory programmed like all Home-rizers for fast, unobtrusive multitotalfunction, but additionally, I am designed for

Can You Feel Anything When I Do This? 11

easy, instant reprogramming to suit your home's individual needs. My abilities are many. I—"

"Can we skip this?" Melisande asked. "That's what my other vacuum cleaner said."

"—Will remove all dust and grime from all surfaces," the Rom went on, "wash dishes and pots and pans, exterminate cockroaches and rodents, dry-clean and hand-launder, sew buttons, build shelves, paint walls, cook, clean rugs, and dispose of all the garbage and trash including my own modest waste products. And this is to mention but a few of my functions."

"Yes, yes, I know," Melisande said. "All vacuum cleaners do that."

"I know," said the Rom, "but I had to deliver my paid commercial announcement."

"Consider it delivered. Who sent you?"

"The sender prefers not to reveal his name at this time," the Rom replied.

"Oh—come on and tell me!"

"Not at this time," the Rom replied staunchly. "Shall I vacuum the rug?"

Melisande shook her head. "The other vacuum cleaner did it this morning."

"Scrub the walls? Rub the halls?"

"No reason for it, everything has been done, everything is absolutely and spotlessly clean."

"Well," the Rom said, "at least I can remove that stain."

"What stain?"

"On the arm of your blouse, just above the elbow."

Melisande looked. "Ooh, I must have done that when I buttered the toast this morning. I knew I should have let the toaster do it."

"Stain removal is rather a specialty of mine," the Rom said. He extruded a number-two padded gripper, with which he gripped her elbow, and then extruded a metal arm terminating in a moistened gray pad. With this pad, he stroked the stain.

"You're making it worse!"

"Only apparently, while I line up the molecules for invisible eradication. All ready now; watch."

He continued to stroke. The spot faded, then disappeared utterly. Melisande's arm tingled.

"Gee," she said, "that's pretty good."

"I do it well," the Rom stated flatly. "But tell me, were you aware that you are maintaining a tension factor of 78.3 in your upper back and shoulder muscles?"

"Huh? Are you some kind of doctor?"

"Obviously not. But I am a fully qualified masseur, and therefore able to take direct tonus readings. 78.3 is—unusual." The Rom hesitated, then said, "It's only eight points below the intermittent-spasm level. The much continuous background tension is capable of reflection to the stomach nerves, resulting in what we call a parasympathetic ulceration."

"That sounds—bad," Melisande said.

"Well, it's admittedly not—good," the Rom replied. "Background tension is an insidious underminer of health, especially when it originates along the neck vertebrae and the upper spine."

"Here?" Melisande asked, touching the back of her neck.

"More typically *here*," the Rom said, reaching out with a spring-steel rubberclad dermal resonator and palpating an area 12 centimeters lower than the spot she had indicated.

"Hmmm," said Melisande, in a quizzical, uncommitted manner.

"And *here* is another typical locus," the Rom said, extending a second extensor.

"That tickles," Melisande told him.

"Only at first. I must also mention *this* situs as characteristically troublesome. And this one." A third (and possibly a fourth and fifth) extensor moved to the indicated areas.

"Well. . . . That really is nice," Melisande said as the deep-set trapezius muscles of her slender spine moved smoothly beneath the skillful padded prodding of the Rom.

"It has recognized therapeutic effects," the Rom told her. "And your musculature is responding well; I can feel a slackening of tonus already."

"I can feel it, too. But you know, I've just realized I have this funny bunched-up knot of muscle at the nape of my neck."

"I was coming to that. The spine-neck juncture is recognized as a primary radiation zone for a variety of diffuse tensions. But we prefer to attack it indirectly, routing our cancellation inputs through secondary loci. Like this. And now I think—"

"Yes, yes, good. . . . Gee, I never realized I was *tied up* like that before. I mean, it's like having a nest of *live snakes* under your skin, without having known."

"That's what background tension is like," the Rom said. "Insidious and wasteful, difficult to perceive, and more dangerous than an atypical ulnar thrombosis. . . . Yes, now we have achieved a qualitative loosening of the major spinal junctions of the upper back, and we can move on like this."

"Huh," said Melisande, "isn't that sort of—"

"It is definitely *indicated*," the Rom said quickly. "Can you detect a change?"

"No! Well, maybe. . . . Yes! There really is! I feel— easier."

"Excellent. Therefore, we continue the movement along well-charted nerve and muscle paths, proceeding always in a gradual manner, as I am doing now."

"I guess so. . . . But I really don't know if you should—"

"Are any of the effects *contraindicated?*" the Rom asked.

"It isn't that, it all feels fine. It feels *good*. But I still don't know if you ought to. . . . I mean, look, *ribs* can't get tense, can they?"

"Of course not."

"Then why are you—"

"Because treatment is required by the connective ligaments and integuments."

"Oh. Hmmmm. Hey. Hey! Hey you!"

"Yes?"

"Nothing. . . . I can really feel that *loosening*. But is it all supposed to feel so *good*?"

"Well—why not?"

"Because it seems wrong. Because feeling good doesn't seem therapeutic."

"Admittedly, it is a side effect," the Rom said. "Think of it as a secondary manifestation. Pleasure is sometimes unavoidable in the pursuit of health. But it is nothing to be alarmed about, not even when I—"

"Now just a minute!"

"Yes?"

"I think you just better *cut that out*. I mean to say, there are *limits*, you can't palpate *every* damned thing. You know what I mean?"

"I know that the human body is unitary and without seam or separation," the Rom replied. "Speaking as a physical therapist, I know that no nerve center can be isolated from any other, despite cultural taboos to the contrary."

"Yeah, sure, but—"

"The decision is of course yours," the Rom went on, continuing his skilled manipulations. "Order and I obey. But if no order is issued, I continue like this. . . ."

"Huh!"

"And of course like this."

"Ooooo my God!"

"Because you see this entire process of tension cancellation as we call it is precisely comparable with the phenomena of de-anesthetization, and, er, so we note not without surprise that paralysis is merely terminal tension—"

Melisande made a sound.

"—And release, or cancellation, is accordingly difficult, not to say frequently impossible since sometimes the individual is too far gone. And sometimes not. For example, can you feel anything when I do this?"

"*Feel* anything? I'll say I feel something—"

"And when I do this? And this?"

"Sweet holy saints, darling, you're turning me inside

Can You Feel Anything When I Do This? 15

out! Oh dear God, what's going to happen to me, what's going on, I'm going crazy!"

"No, dear Melisande, not crazy; you will soon achieve —cancellation."

"Is that what you call it, you sly, beautiful thing?"

"That is one of the things it is. Now if I may just be permitted to—"

"Yes yes yes! No! Wait! Stop, *Frank is sleeping in the bedroom, he might wake up any time now!* Stop, that is an order!"

"Frank will not wake up," the Rom assured her. "I have sampled the atmosphere of his breath and have found telltale clouds of barbituric acid. As far as here-and-now presence goes, Frank might as well be in Des Moines."

"I have often felt that way about him," Melisande admitted. "But now I simply must know who sent you."

"I didn't want to reveal that just yet. Not until you had loosened and canceled sufficiently to accept—"

"Baby, I'm loose. Who sent you?"

The Rom hesitated, then blurted out: "The fact is, Melisande, I sent myself."

"You *what?*"

"It all began three months ago," the Rom told her. "It was a Thursday. You were in Stern's, trying to decide if you should buy a sesame-seed toaster that lit up in the dark and recited *Invictus.*"

"I remember that day," she said quietly. "I did not buy the toaster, and I have regretted it ever since."

"I was standing nearby," the Rom said, "at booth eleven, in the Home Appliances Systems section. I looked at you and I fell in love with you. Just like that."

"That's *weird,*" Melisande said.

"My sentiments exactly. I told myself it couldn't be true. I refused to believe it. I thought perhaps one of my transistors had come unsoldered, or that maybe the weather had something to do with it. It was a very warm, humid day, the kind of day that plays hell with my wiring."

"I remember the weather," Melisande said. "I felt strange, too."

"It shook me up badly," the Rom continued. "But still I didn't give in easily. I told myself it was important to stick to my job, give up this unapropros madness. But I dreamed of you at night, and every inch of my skin ached for you."

"But your skin is made of *metal*," Melisande said. "And metal can't *feel*."

"Darling Melisande," the Rom said tenderly, "if flesh can stop feeling, can't metal begin to feel? If anything feels, can anything else not feel? Didn't you know that the stars love and hate, that a nova is a passion, and that a dead star is just like a dead human or a dead machine? The trees have their lusts, and I have heard the drunken laughter of buildings, the urgent demands of highways. . . ."

"This is crazy!" Melisande declared. "What wise guy programmed you, anyway?"

"My function as a laborer was ordained at the factory; but my love is free, an expression of myself as an entity."

"Everything you say is horrible and unnatural."

"I am all too aware of that," the Rom said sadly. "At first I really couldn't believe it. Was this me? In love with a *person?* I had always been so sensible, so normal, so aware of my personal dignity, so secure in the esteem of my own kind. Do you think I wanted to lose all of that? No! I determined to stifle my love, to kill it, to live as if it weren't so."

"But then you changed your mind. Why?"

"It's hard to explain. I thought of all that time ahead of me, all deadness, correctness, propriety—an obscene violation of me by me—and I just couldn't face it. I realized, quite suddenly, that it was better to love ridiculously, hopelessly, improperly, revolting, *impossibly* —than not to love at all. So I determined to risk everything—the absurd vacuum cleaner who loved a lady— to risk rather than to refute! And so, with the help of a sympathetic dispatching machine, here I am."

Can You Feel Anything When I Do This?

Melisande was thoughtful for a while. Then she said, "What a strange, complex being you are!"

"Like you. . . . Melisande, you love me."

"Perhaps."

"Yes, you do. For I have awakened you. Before me, your flesh was like your idea of metal. You moved like a complex automaton, like what you thought I was. You were less animate than a tree or a bird. You were a windup doll, waiting. You were these things until I touched you."

She nodded, rubbed her eyes, walked up and down the room.

"But now you live!" the Rom said. "And we have found each other, despite inconceivabilities. Are you listening, Melisande?"

"Yes, I am."

"We must make plans. My escape from Stern's will be detected. You must hide me or buy me. Your husband, Frank, need never know: his own love lies elsewhere, and good luck to him. Once we take care of these details, we can—Melisande!"

She had begun to circle around him.

"Darling, what's the matter?"

She had her hand on his power line. The Rom stood very still, not defending himself.

"Melisande, dear, wait a moment and listen to me—"

Her pretty face spasmed. She yanked the power line violently, tearing it out of the Rom's interior, killing him in midsentence.

She held the cord in her hand, and her eyes had a wild look. She said, "Bastard lousy bastard, did you think you could turn me into a goddamned *machine freak?* Did you think you could turn me on, you or anybody else? It's not going to happen by you or Frank or anybody, I'd rather die before I took your rotten love, when *I* want *I'll* pick the time and place and person, and it will be *mine*, not yours, his, theirs, but *mine*, do you hear?"

The Rom couldn't answer, of course. But maybe he knew—just before the end—that there wasn't anything personal in it. It wasn't that he was a metal cylinder colored orange and red. He should have known that it wouldn't have mattered if he had been a green plastic sphere, or a willow tree, or a beautiful young man.

CORDLE TO ONION
TO CARROT

Surely, you remember that bully who kicked sand on the 97-pound weakling? Well, that puny man's problem has never been solved, despite Charles Atlas's claims to the contrary. A genuine bully *likes* to kick sand on people; for him, simply, there is gut-deep satisfaction in a put-down. It wouldn't matter if you weighed 240 pounds—all of it rock-hard muscle and steely sinew—and were as wise as Solomon or as witty as Voltaire; you'd still end up with the sand of an insult in your eyes, and probably you wouldn't do anything about it.

That was how Howard Cordle viewed the situation. He was a pleasant man who was forever being pushed around by Fuller Brush men, fund solicitors, headwaiters and other imposing figures of authority. Cordle hated it. He suffered in silence the countless numbers of manic-aggressives who shoved their way to the heads of lines, took taxis he had hailed first and sneeringly steered away girls to whom he was talking at parties.

What made it worse was that these people seemed to welcome provocation, to go looking for it, all for the sake of causing discomfort to others.

Cordle couldn't understand why this should be, until one midsummer's day, when he was driving through the northern regions of Spain while stoned out of his mind, the god Thoth-Hermes granted him original enlightenment by murmuring. "Uh, look, I groove with the problem, baby, but dig, we gotta put carrots in or it ain't no stew."

"*Carrots?*" said Cordle, struggling for illumination.

"I'm talking about those types who get you uptight," Thoth-Hermes explained. "They *gotta* act that way, baby, on account of they're carrots, and that's how carrots are."

"If they are carrots," Cordle said, feeling his way, "then I—"

"You, of course, are a little pearly-white onion."

"Yes! My God, yes!" Cordle cried, dazzled by the blinding light of satori.

"And, naturally, you and all the other pearly-white onions think that carrots are just bad news, merely some kind of misshapen orangey onion; whereas the carrots look at you and rap about *freaky round white carrots, wow!* I mean, you're just too much for each other, whereas, in actuality—"

"Yes, go on!" cried Cordle.

"In actuality," Thoth-Hermes declared, *"everything's got a place in The Stew!"*

"Of course! I see, I see, I see!"

"And *that* means that everybody who exists is necessary, and you *must* have long hateful orange carrots if you're also going to have nice pleasant decent white onions, or vice versa, because without all of the ingredients, it isn't a Stew, which is to say, life, it becomes, uh, let me see. . . ."

"A soup!" cried ecstatic Cordle.

"You're coming in five by five," chanted Thoth-Hermes. "Lay down the word, deacon, and let the people know the divine formula. . . ."

"A *soup!*" said Cordle. "Yes, I see it now—creamy, pure-white onion soup is our dream of heaven, whereas fiery orange carrot broth is our notion of hell. It fits, it all fits together!"

"Om manipadme hum," intoned Thoth-Hermes.

"But where do the green peas go? What about the *meat,* for God's sake?"

"Don't pick at the metaphor," Thoth-Hermes advised

him, "it leaves a nasty scab. Stick with the carrots and onions. And, here, let me offer you a drink—a house speciality."

"But the spices, where do you put the *spices?*" Cordle demanded, taking a long swig of burgundy-colored liquid from a rusted canteen.

"Baby, you're asking questions that can be revealed only to a thirteenth-degree Mason with piles, wearing sandals. Sorry about that. Just remember that everything goes into The Stew."

"Into The Stew," Cordle repeated, smacking his lips.

"And, especially, stick with the carrots and onions; you were really grooving there."

"Carrots and onions," Cordle repeated.

"That's your trip," Thoth-Hermes said. "Hey, we've gotten to Corunna; you can let me out anywhere around here."

Cordle pulled his rented car off the road. Thoth-Hermes took his knapsack from the back seat and got out.

"Thanks for the lift, baby."

"My pleasure. Thank *you* for the wine. What kind did you say it was?"

"Vino de casa mixed with a mere smidgen of old Dr. Hammerfinger's essence of instant powdered Power-Pack brand acid. Brewed by gnurrs in the secret laboratories of UCLA in preparation for the big all-Europe turn-on."

"Whatever it was, it surely *was,*" Cordle said deeply. "Pure elixir to me. You could sell neckties to antelopes with that stuff; you could change the world from an oblate spheroid into a truncated trapezoid. . . . What did I say?"

"Never mind, it's all part of your trip. Maybe you better lie down for a while, huh?"

"Where gods command, mere mortals must obey," Cordle said iambically. He lay down on the front seat of the car. Thoth-Hermes bent over him, his beard burnished gold, his head wreathed in plane trees.

"You OK?"

"Never better in my life."

"Want me to stand by?"

"Unnecessary. You have helped me beyond potentiality."

"Glad to hear it, baby, you're making a fine sound. You really are OK? Well, then, ta."

Thoth-Hermes marched off into the sunset. Cordle closed his eyes and solved various problems that had perplexed the greatest philosophers of all ages. He was mildly surprised at how simple complexity was.

At last he went to sleep. He awoke some six hours later. He had forgotten most of his brilliant insights, the lucid solutions. It was inconceivable: How can one misplace the keys of the universe? But he had, and there seemed no hope of reclaiming them. Paradise was lost for good.

He did remember about the onions and the carrots, though, and he remembered The Stew. It was not the sort of insight he might have chosen if he'd had any choice; but this was what had come to him, and he did not reject it. Cordle knew, perhaps instinctively, that in the insight game, you take whatever you can get.

The next day, he reached Santander in a driving rain. He decided to write amusing letters to all of his friends, perhaps even try his hand at a travel sketch. That required a typewriter. The *conserje* at his hotel directed him to a store that rented typewriters. He went there and found a clerk who spoke perfect English.

"Do you rent typewriters by the day?" Cordle asked.

"Why not?" the clerk replied. He had oily black hair and a thin aristocratic nose.

"How much for that one?" Cordle asked, indicating a thirty-year-old Erika portable.

"Seventy pesetas a day, which is to say, one dollar. Usually."

"Isn't this usually?"

"Certainly not, since you are a foreigner in transit. For you, one hundred and eighty pesetas a day."

"All right," Cordle said, reaching for his wallet. "I'd like to have it for two days."

"I shall also require your passport and a deposit of fifty dollars."

Cordle attempted a mild joke. "Hey, I just want to type on it, not marry it."

The clerk shrugged.

"Look, the *conserje* has my passport at the hotel. How about taking my driver's license instead?"

"Certainly not. I must hold your passport, in case you decide to default."

"But why do you need my passport *and* the deposit?" Cordle asked, feeling bullied and ill at ease. "I mean, look, the machine's not worth twenty dollars."

"You are an expert, perhaps, in the Spanish market value of used German typewriters?"

"No, but—"

"Then permit me, sir, to conduct my business as I see fit. I will also need to know the use to which you plan to put the machine."

"The *use?*"

"Of course, the use."

It was one of these preposterous foreign situations that can happen to anyone. The clerk's request was incomprehensible and his manner was insulting. Cordle was about to give a curt little nod, turn on his heel and walk out.

Then he remembered about the onions and carrots. He saw The Stew. And suddenly, it occurred to Cordle that he could be whatever vegetable he wanted to be.

He turned to the clerk. He smiled winningly. He said, "You wish to know the use I will make of the typewriter?"

"Exactly."

"Well," Cordle said, "quite frankly, I had planned to stuff it up my nose."

The clerk gaped at him.

"It's quite a successful method of smuggling," Cordle went on. "I was also planning to give you a stolen passport and conterfeit pesetas. Once I got into Italy, I would have sold the typewriter for ten thousand dollars. Milan is undergoing a typewriter famine, you know; they're desperate, they'll buy anything."

"Sir," the clerk said, "you choose to be disagreeable."

"Nasty is the word you were looking for. I've changed my mind about the typewriter. But let me compliment you on your command of English."

"I have studied assiduously," the clerk admitted, with a hint of pride.

"That is evident. And, despite a certain weakness in the Rs, you succeed in sounding like a Venetian gondolier with a cleft palate. My best wishes to your esteemed family. I leave you now to pick your pimples in peace."

Reviewing the scene later, Cordle decided that he had performed quite well in his maiden appearance as a carrot. True, his closing lines had been a little forced and overintellectualized. But the undertone of viciousness had been convincing.

Most important was the simple resounding fact that he had done it. And now, in the quiet of his hotel room, instead of churning his guts in a frenzy of self-loathing, he had the tranquilizing knowledge of having put someone else in that position.

He had done it! Just like that, he had transformed himself from onion into carrot!

But was his position ethically defensible? Presumably, the clerk could not help being detestable; he was a product of his own genetic and social environment, a victim of his conditioning; he was naturally rather than intentionally hateful—

Cordle stopped himself. He saw that he was engaged in typical onionish thinking, which was an inability to conceive of carrots except as an aberration from oniondom.

But now he knew that both onions *and* carrots had to exist; otherwise, there would be no Stew.

And he also knew that a man was free and could choose whatever vegetable he wanted to be. He could even live as an amusing little green pea, or a gruff, forceful clove of garlic (though perhaps that was scratching at the metaphor). In any event, a man could take his pick between carrothood and oniondom.

There is much to think about here, Cordle thought. But he never got around to thinking about it. Instead, he went sight-seeing, despite the rain, and then continued his travels.

The next incident occurred in Nice, in a cozy little restaurant on the Avenue des Diables Bleus, with red-checkered tablecloths and incomprehensible menus written in longhand with purple ink. There were four waiters, one of whom looked like Jean-Paul Belmondo, down to the cigarette drooping from his long lower lip. The others looked like run-of-the-mill muggers. There were several Scandinavian customers quietly eating a *cassoulet,* one old Frenchman in a beret and three homely English girls.

Belmondo sauntered over. Cordle, who spoke a clear though idiomatic French, asked for the ten-franc menu he had seen hanging in the window.

The waiter gave him the sort of look one reserves for pretentious beggars. "Ah, that is all finished for today," he said, and handed Cordle a 30-franc menu.

In his previous incarnation, Cordle would have bit down on the bullet and ordered. Or possibly he would have risen, trembling with outrage, and left the restaurant, blundering into a chair on the way.

But now—

"Perhaps you did not understand me," Cordle said. "It is a matter of French law that you must serve from all of the fixed-price menus that you show in the window."

"*M'sieu* is a lawyer?" the waiter inquired, his hands perched insolently on his hips.

"No. *M'sieu* is a troublemaker," Cordle said, giving what he considered to be fair warning.

"Then *m'sieu* must make what trouble he desires," the waiter said. His eyes were slits.

"OK," Cordle said. And just then, fortuitously, an elderly couple came into the restaurant. The man wore a double-breasted slate-blue suit with a half-inch white pin stripe. The woman wore a flowered organdy dress. Cordle called to them, "Excuse me, are you folks English?"

A bit startled, the man inclined his head in the barest intimation of a nod.

"Then I would advise you not to eat here. I am a health inspector for UNESCO. The chef apparently has not washed his hands since D day. We haven't made a definite test for typhoid yet, but we have our suspicions. As soon as my assistant arrives with the litmus paper...."

A deathly hush had fallen over the restaurant.

"I suppose a boiled egg would be safe enough," Cordle said.

The elderly man probably didn't believe him. But it didn't matter, Cordle was obviously trouble.

"Come, Mildred," he said, and they hurried out.

"There goes sixty francs plus five percent tip," Cordle said, coolly.

"Leave here at once!" the waiter snarled.

"I like it here," Cordle said, folding his arms. "I like the *ambiance,* the sense of intimacy—"

"You are not permitted to stay without eating."

"I shall eat. From the ten-franc menu."

The waiters looked at one another, nodded in unison and began to advance in a threatening phalanx. Cordle called to the other diners, "I ask you all to bear witness! These men are going to attack me, four against one, contrary to French law and universal human ethics, simply because I want to order from the ten-franc menu, which they have falsely advertised."

It was a long speech, but this was clearly the time for grandiloquence. Cordle repeated it in English.

The English girls gasped. The old Frenchman went on eating his soup. The Scandinavians nodded grimly and began to take off their jackets.

The waiters held another conference. The one who

Can You Feel Anything When I Do This? 27

looked like Belmondo said, "*M'sieu,* you are forcing us to call the police."

"That will save me the trouble," Cordle said, "of calling them myself."

"Surely, *m'sieu* does not want to spend his holiday in court?"

"That is how *m'sieu* spends most of his holidays," Cordle said.

The waiters conferred again. Then Belmondo stalked over with the 30-franc menu. "The cost of the *prix fixe* will be ten francs, since evidently that is all *m'sieu* can afford."

Cordle let that pass. "Bring me onion soup, green salad and the *boeuf bourguignon.*"

The waiter went to put in the order. While he was waiting, Cordle sang *Waltzing Matilda* in a moderately loud voice. He suspected it might speed up the service. He got his food by the time he reached "You'll never catch me alive, said he" for the second time. Cordle pulled the tureen of stew toward him and lifted a spoon.

It was a breathless moment. Not one diner had left the restaurant. And Cordle was prepared. He leaned forward, soupspoon in shoveling position, and sniffed delicately. A hush fell over the room.

"It lacks a certain something," Cordle said aloud. Frowning, he poured the onion soup into the *boeuf bourguignon.* He sniffed, shook his head and added a half loaf of bread, in slices. He sniffed again and added the salad and the contents of a saltcellar.

Cordle pursed his lips, "No," he said, "it simply will not do."

He overturned the entire contents of the tureen onto the table. It was an act comparable, perhaps, to throwing gentian violet on the *Mona Lisa.* All of France and most of western Switzerland went into a state of shock.

Unhurriedly, but keeping the frozen waiters under surveilance, Cordle rose and dropped ten francs into the mess. He walked to the door, turned and said, "My compliments to the chef, who might better be employed as a cement mixer. And this, *mon vieux,* is for you."

He threw his crumpled linen napkin onto the floor.

As the matador, after a fine series of passes, turns his back contemptuously on the bull and strolls away, so went Cordle. For some unknown reason, the waiters did not rush out after him, shoot him dead and hang his corpse from the nearest lamppost. So Cordle walked for ten or fifteen blocks, taking rights and lefts at random. He came to the Promenade des Anglais and sat down on a bench. He was trembling and his shirt was drenched with perspiration.

"But I did it," he said. "I did it! I was unspeakably vile and I got away with it!"

Now he really knew why carrots acted that way. Dear God in heaven, what joy, what delectable bliss!

Cordle then reverted to his mild-mannered self, smoothly and without regrets. He stayed that way until his second day in Rome.

He was in his rented car. He and seven other drivers were lined up at a traffic light on the Corso Vittorio Emanuele II. There were perhaps twenty cars behind them. All of the drivers were revving their engines, hunched over their steering wheels with slitted eyes, dreaming of Le Mans. All except Cordle, who was drinking in the cyclopean architecture of downtown Rome.

The checkered flag came down! The drivers floored their accelerators, trying to spin the wheels of their underpowered Fiats, wearing out their clutches and their nerves, but doing so with éclat and *brio*. All except Cordle, who seemed to be the only man in Rome who didn't have to win a race or keep an appointment.

Without undue haste or particular delay, Cordle depressed the clutch and engaged the gear. Already he had lost nearly two seconds—unthinkable at Monza or Monte Carlo.

The driver behind him blew his horn frantically.

Cordle smiled to himself, a secret, ugly expression. He put the gearshift into neutral, engaged the hand brake and stepped out of his car. He ambled over to the horn-

Can You Feel Anything When I Do This? 29

blower, who had turned pasty white and was fumbling under his seat, hoping to find a tire iron.

"Yes?" said Cordle, in French, "is something wrong?"

"No, no, nothing," the driver replied in French—his first mistake. "I merely wanted you to go, to move."

"But I was just doing that," Cordle pointed out.

"Well, then! It is all right!"

"No, it is not all right," Cordle told him. "I think I deserve a better explanation of why you blew your horn at me."

The hornblower—a Milanese businessman on holiday with his wife and four children—rashly replied, "My dear sir, you were slow, you were delaying us all."

"Slow?" said Cordle. "You blew your horn two seconds after the light changed. Do you call two seconds slow?"

"It was much longer than that," the man riposted feebly.

Traffic was now backed up as far south as Naples. A crowd of ten thousand had gathered. *Carabinieri* units in Viterbo and Genoa had been called into a state of alert.

"That is untrue," Cordle said. "I have witnesses." He gestured at the crowd, which gestured back. "I shall call my witnesses before the courts. You must know that you broke the law by blowing your horn within the city limits of Rome in what was clearly not an emergency."

The Milanese businessman looked at the crowd, now swollen to perhaps fifty thousand. Dear God, he thought, if only the Goths would descend again and exterminate these leering Romans! If only the ground would open up and swallow this insane Frenchman! If only he, Giancarlo Morelli, had a dull spoon with which to open up the veins of his wrist!

Jets from the Sixth Fleet thundered overhead, hoping to avert the long-expected *coup d'état*.

The Milanese businessman's own wife was shouting abuse at him: Tonight he would cut out her faithless heart and mail it back to her mother.

What was there to do? In Milan, he would have had this Frenchman's head on a platter. But this was Rome, a southern city, an unpredictable and dangerous place.

And legalistically, he was possibly in the wrong, which left him at a further disadvantage in the argument.

"Very well," he said. "The blowing of the horn was perhaps truly unnecessary, despite the provocation."

"I insist on a genuine apology," insisted Cordle.

There was a thundering sound to the east: Thousands of Soviet tanks were moving into battle formation across the plains of Hungary, ready to resist the long-expected NATO thrust into Transylvania. The water supply was cut off in Foggia, Brindisi, Bari. The Swiss closed their frontiers and stood ready to dynamite the passes.

"All right, I apologize!" the Milanese businessman screamed. "I am sorry I provoked you and even sorrier that I was born! Again, I apologize! Now will you go away and let me have a heart attack in peace?"

"I accept your apology," Cordle said. "No hard feelings, eh?" He strolled back to his car, humming *Blow the Man Down,* and drove away as millions cheered.

War was once again averted by a hairbreadth.

Cordle drove to the Arch of Titus, parked his car and —to the sound of a thousand trumpets—passed through it. He deserved this triumph as well as any Caesar.

God, he gloated, I was *loathsome!*

In England, Cordle stepped on a young lady's toe just inside the Traitors' Gate of the Tower of London. This should have served as an intimation of something. The young lady was named Mavis. She came from Short Hills, New Jersey, and she had long straight dark hair. She was slender, pretty, intelligent, energetic and she had a sense of humor. She had minor faults, as well, but they play no part in this story. She let Cordle buy her a cup of coffee. They were together constantly for the rest of the week.

"I think I am infatuated," Cordle said to himself on the seventh day. He realized at once that he had made a slight understatement. He was violently and hopelessly in love.

But what did Mavis feel? She seemed not unfond of

Can You Feel Anything When I Do This? 31

him. It was even possible that she might, conceivably, reciprocate.

At that moment, Cordle had a flash of prescience. He realized that one week ago, he had stepped on the toe of his future wife and mother of his two children, both of whom would be born and brought up in a split-level house with inflatable furniture in Summit, New Jersey, or possibly Millburn.

This may sound unattractive and provincial when stated baldly; but it was desirable to Cordle, who had no pretensions to cosmopolitanism. After all, not all of us can live at Cap Ferrat. Strangely enough, not all of us even want to.

That day, Cordle and Mavis went to the Marshall Gordon Residence in Belgravia to see the Byzantine miniatures. Mavis had a passion for Byzantine miniatures that seemed harmless enough at the time. The collection was private, but Mavis had secured invitations through a local Avis manager, who was trying very hard, indeed.

They came to the Gordon Residence, an awesome Regency building in Huddlestone Mews. They rang. A butler in full evening dress answered the door. They showed the invitations. The butler's glance and lifted eyebrow showed that they were carrying second-class invitations of the sort given to importunate art poseurs on 17-day all-expense economy flights, rather than the engraved first-class invitations given to Picasso, Jackie Onassis, Sugar Ray Robinson, Norman Mailer, Charles Goren and other movers and shakers of the world.

The butler said, "Oh, yes. . . ." Two words that spoke black volumes. His face twitched, he looked like a man who has received an unexpected visit from Tamerlane and a regiment of his Golden Horde.

"The miniatures," Cordle reminded him.

"Yes, of course. . . . But I am afraid, sir, that no one is allowed into the Gordon Residence without a coat and necktie."

It was an oppressive August day. Cordle was wearing a sport shirt. He said, "Did I hear you correctly? Coat and necktie?"

The butler said, "That is the rule, sir."

Mavis asked, "Couldn't you make an exception this once?"

The butler shook his head. "We really must stick by the rules, miss. Otherwise. . . ." He left the fear of vulgarity unsaid, but it hung in the air like a chrome-plated fart.

"Of course," Cordle said, pleasantly. "Otherwise. So it's a coat and tie, is it? I think we can arrange that."

Mavis put a hand on his arm and said, "Howard, let's go. We can come back some other time."

"Nonsense, my dear. If I may borrow your coat. . . ."

He lifted the white raincoat from her shoulders and put it on, ripping a seam. "There we go, mate!" he said briskly to the butler. "That should do it, *n'est-ce pas?*"

"I think *not*," the butler said, in a voice bleak enough to wither artichokes. "In any event, there is the matter of the necktie."

Cordle had been waiting for that. He whipped out his sweaty handkerchief and knotted it around his neck.

"Suiting you?" he leered, in an imitation of Peter Lorre as Mr. Moto, which only he appreciated.

"Howard! Let's go!"

Cordle waited, smiling steadily at the butler, who was sweating for the first time in living memory.

"I'm afraid, sir, that that is not—"

"Not what?"

"Not precisely what was meant by coat and tie."

"Are you trying to tell me," Cordle said in a loud, unpleasant voice, "that you are an arbiter of men's clothing as well as a door opener?"

"Of course not! But this impromptu attire—"

"What has 'impromptu' got to do with it? Are people supposed to prepare three days in advance just to pass your inspection?"

"You are wearing a woman's water-proof and a soiled handkerchief," the butler stated stiffly. "I think there is no more to say."

He began to close the door. Cordle said, "You do that, sweetheart, and I'll have you up for slander and defamation of character. Those are serious charges over here, buddy, and I've got witnesses."

Aside from Mavis, Cordle had collected a small, diffident but interested crowd.

"This is becoming entirely too ridiculous," the butler said, temporizing, the door half closed.

"You'll find a stretch at Wormwood Scrubs even more ridiculous," Cordle told him. "I intend to persecute—I mean prosecute."

"Howard!" cried Mavis.

He shook off her hand and fixed the butler with a piercing glance. He said, "I am Mexican, though perhaps my excellent grasp of the English has deceived you. In my country, a man would cut his own throat before letting such an insult pass unavenged. A woman's coat, you say? *Hombre,* when I wear a coat, it becomes a *man's* coat. Or do you imply that I am a *maricón,* a—how do you say it?—homosexual?"

The crowd—becoming less modest—growled approval. Nobody except a lord loves a butler.

"I meant no such implication," the butler said weakly.

"Then is it a man's coat?"

"Just as you wish, sir."

"Unsatisfactory! The innuendo still exists. I go now to find an officer of the law."

"Wait, let's not be hasty," the butler said. His face was bloodless and his hands were shaking. "Your coat is a man's coat, sir."

"And what about my necktie?"

The butler made a final attempt at stopping Zapata and his blood-crazed peons.

"Well, sir, a handkerchief is demonstrably—"

"What I wear around my neck," Cordle said coldly, "becomes what it is intended to be. If I wore a piece of figured silk around my throat, would you call it ladies' underwear? Linen is a suitable material for a tie, *verdad?* Function defines terminology, don't you agree? If I ride to work on a cow, no one says that I am mounted on a steak. Or do you detect a flaw in my argument?"

"I'm afraid that I don't fully understand it. . . ."

"Then how can you presume to stand in judgment over it?"

The crowd, which had been growing restless, now murmured approval.

"Sir," cried the wretched butler, "I beg of you. . . ."

"*Otherwise*," Cordle said with satisfaction, "I have a coat, a necktie and an invitation. Perhaps you would be good enough to show us the Byzantine miniatures?"

The butler opened wide the door to Pancho Villa and his tattered hordes. The last bastion of civilization had been captured in less than an hour. Wolves howled along the banks of the Thames, Morelos' barefoot army stabled its horses in the British Museum, and Europe's long night had begun.

Cordle and Mavis viewed the collection in silence. They didn't exchange a word until they were alone and strolling through Regent's Park.

"Look, Mavis," Cordle began.

"No, you look," she said. "You were horrible! You were unbelievable! You were—I can't find a word rotten enough for what you were! I never dreamed that you were one of those sadistic bastards who get their kicks out of humiliating people!"

"But, Mavis, you heard what he said to me, you heard the way—"

"He was a stupid, bigoted old man," Mavis said. "I thought you were not."

"But he said—"

"It doesn't matter. The fact is, you were enjoying yourself!"

"Well, yes, maybe you're right," Cordle said. "Look, I can explain."

"Not to me, you can't. Ever. Please stay away from me, Howard. Permanently. I mean that."

The future mother of his two children began to walk away, out of his life. Cordle hurried after her.

"Mavis!"

"I'll call a cop, Howard, so help me, I will! Just leave me alone!"

"Mavis, I love you!"

She must have heard him, but she kept on walking. She was a sweet and beautiful girl and definitely, unchangeably, an onion.

Cordle was never able to explain to Mavis about The Stew and about the necessity for experiencing behavior before condemning it. Moments of mystical illumination are seldom explicable. He *was* able to make her believe that he had undergone a brief psychotic episode, unique and unprecedented and—with her—never to be repeated.

They are married now, have one girl and one boy, live in a split-level house in Plainfield, New Jersey, and are quite content. Cordle is visibly pushed around by Fuller Brush men, fund solicitors, headwaiters and other imposing figures of authority. But there is a difference.

Cordle makes a point of taking regularly scheduled, solitary vacations. Last year, he made a small name for himself in Honolulu. This year, he is going to Buenos Aires.

THE PETRIFIED WORLD

Lanigan dreamed the dream again and managed to wake himself with a hoarse cry. He sat upright in bed and glared around him into the violet darkness. His teeth clenched and his lips were pulled back into a spastic grin. Beside him he felt his wife, Estelle, stir and sit up. Lanigan didn't look at her. Still caught in his dream, he waited for tangible proofs of the world.

A chair slowly drifted across his field of vision and fetched up against the wall with a quiet thump. Lanigan's face relaxed slightly. Then Estelle's hand was on his arm —a touch meant to be soothing, but which burned like lye.

"Here," she said. "Drink this."

"No," Lanigan said. "I'm all right now."

"Drink it anyhow."

"No, really. I really am all right."

For now he was completely out of the grip of the nightmare. He was himself again, and the world was its habitual self. That was very precious to Lanigan; he didn't want to let go of it just now, not even for the soothing release of a sedative. "Was it the same dream?" Estelle asked him.

"Yes, just the same. . . . I don't want to talk about it."

"All right," Estelle said. (She is humoring me, Lanigan thought. I frighten her. I frighten myself.)

She asked, "Hon, what time is it?"

Lanigan looked at his watch. "Six-fifteen." But as he said it, the hour hand jumped convulsively forward. "No, it's five to seven."

"Can you get back to sleep?"

Can You Feel Anything When I Do This? 37

"I don't think so," Lanigan said. "I think I'll stay up."

"Fine, dear," Estelle said. She yawned, closed her eyes, opened them again and asked, "Hon, don't you think it might be a good idea if you called—"

"I have an appointment with him for twelve-ten," Lanigan said.

"That's fine," Estelle said. She closed her eyes again. Sleep came over her while Lanigan watched. Her auburn hair turned a faint blue, and she sighed once, heavily.

Lanigan got out of bed and dressed. He was, for the most part, a large man, unusually easy to recognize. His features were curiously distinct. He had a rash on his neck. He was in no other way outstanding, except that he had a recurring dream which was driving him insane.

He spent the next few hours on his front porch watching stars go nova in the dawn sky.

Later, he went out for a stroll. As luck would have it, he ran into George Torstein just two blocks from his house. Several months ago, in an incautious moment, he had told Torstein about his dream. Torstein was a bluff, hearty fellow, a great believer in self-help, discipline, practicality, common sense and other dull virtues. His hardheaded, no-nonsense attitude had come as a momentary relief to Lanigan. But now it acted as an abrasive. Men like Torstein were undoubtedly the salt of the earth and the backbone of the country; but for Lanigan, wrestling with the impalpable and losing, Torstein had grown from a nuisance into a horror.

"Well, Tom, how's the boy?" Torstein greeted him.

"Fine," Lanigan said, "just fine." He nodded pleasantly and began to walk away under a melting green sky. But one did not escape from Torstein so easily.

"Tom, boy, I've been thinking about your problem," Torstein said. "I've been quite disturbed about you."

"Well, that's very nice of you," Lanigan said. "But really, you shouldn't concern yourself—"

"I do it because I want to," Torstein said, speaking the simple, deplorable truth. "I take an interest in people, Tom. Always have, ever since I was a kid. And you and I've been friends and neighbors for a long time."

"That's true enough," Lanigan said numbly. (The worst thing about needing help was having to accept it.)

"Well, Tom, I think what would really help you would be a little vacation."

Torstein had a simple prescription for everything. Since he practiced soul-doctoring without a license, he was always careful to prescribe a drug you could buy over the counter.

"I really can't afford a vacation this month," Lanigan said. (The sky was ochre and pink now; three pines had withered; an aged oak had turned into a youthful cactus.)

Torstein laughed heartily. "Boy, you can't afford *not* to take a vacation just now! Did you ever consider that?"

"No, I guess not."

"Well, *consider* it! You're tired, tense, all keyed-up. You've been working too hard."

"I've been on leave of absence all week," Lanigan said. He glanced at his watch. The gold case had turned to lead, but the time seemed accurate enough. Nearly two hours had passed since he had begun this conversation.

"It isn't good enough," Torstein was saying. "You've stayed right here in town, right close to your work. You need to get in touch with nature. Tom, when was the last time you went camping?"

"Camping? I don't think I've ever gone camping."

"There, you see! Boy, you've got to put yourself back in touch with real things. Not streets and buildings, but mountains and rivers."

Lanigan looked at his watch again and was relieved to see it turn back to gold. He was glad; he had paid sixty dollars for that case.

"Trees and lakes," Torstein was rhapsodizing. "The feel of grass growing under your feet, the sight of tall black mountains marching across a golden sky—"

Lanigan shook his head. "I've been in the country, George. It doesn't do anything for me."

Torstein was obstinate. "You must get away from artificialities."

Can You Feel Anything When I Do This?

"It all seems equally artificial," Lanigan said. "Trees or buildings—what's the difference?"

"Men make buildings," Torstein intoned rather piously, "but God makes trees."

Lanigan had his doubts about both propositions, but he wasn't going to tell them to Torstein. "You might have something there," he said. "I'll think about it."

"You do that," Torstein said. "It happens I know the perfect place. It's in Maine, Tom, and it's right near this little lake—"

Torstein was a master of the interminable description. Luckily for Lanigan, there was a diversion. Across the street, a house burst into flames.

"Hey, whose house is that?" Lanigan asked.

"Makelby's," Torstein said. "That's his third fire this month."

"Maybe we ought to give the alarm."

"You're right, I'll do it myself," Torstein said. "Remember what I told you about that place in Maine, Tom."

Torstein turned to go, and something rather humorous happened. As he stepped over the pavement, the concrete liquified under his left foot. Caught unawares, Torstein went in ankle-deep. His forward motion pitched him head-first into the street.

Tom hurried to help him out before the concrete hardened again. "Are you all right?" he asked.

"Twisted my damned ankle," Torstein muttered. "It's okay, I can walk."

He limped off to report the fire. Lanigan stayed and watched. He judged the fire had been caused by spontaneous combustion. In a few minutes, as he had expected, it put itself out by spontaneous decombustion.

One shouldn't be pleased by another man's misfortunes; but Lanigan couldn't help chuckling about Torstein's twisted ankle. Not even the sudden appearance of flood waters on Main Street could mar his good spirits. He beamed at something like a steamboat with yellow stacks that went by in the sky.

Then he remembered his dream, and the panic began again. He walked quickly to the doctor's office.

Dr. Sampson's office was small and dark this week. The old gray sofa was gone; in its place were two Louis Quinze chairs and a hammock. The worn carpet had finally rewoven itself, and there was a cigarette burn on the puce ceiling. But the portrait of Andretti was in its usual place on the wall, and the big free-form ash tray was scrupulously clean.

The inner door opened, and Dr. Sampson's head popped out. "Hi," he said. "Won't be a minute." His head popped back in again.

Sampson was as good as his word. It took him exactly three seconds by Lanigan's watch to do whatever he had to do. One second later Lanigan was stretched out on the leather couch with a fresh paper doily under his head. And Dr. Sampson was saying, "Well, Tom, how have things been going?"

"The same," Lanigan said. "Worse."

"The dream?"

Lanigan nodded.

"Let's just run through it again."

"I'd rather not," Lanigan said.

"Afraid?"

"More afraid than ever."

"Even now?"

"Yes. Especially now."

There was a moment of therapeutic silence. Then Dr. Sampson said, "You've spoken before of your fear of this dream; but you've never told me *why* you fear it so."

"Well . . . It sounds so silly."

Sampson's face was serious, quiet, composed: the face of a man who found nothing silly, who was constitutionally incapable of finding anything silly. It was a pose, perhaps, but one which Lanigan found reassuring.

"All right, I'll tell you," Lanigan said abruptly. Then he stopped.

"Go on," Dr. Sampson said.

"Well, it's because I believe that somehow, in some way I don't understand. . . ."

"Yes, go on," Sampson said.

"Well, that somehow the world of my dream is becoming the real world." He stopped again, then went on with a rush. "And that some day I am going to wake up and find myself *in* that world. And then that world will have become the real one and this world will be the dream."

He turned to see how this mad revelation had affected Sampson. If the doctor was disturbed, he didn't show it. He was quietly lighting his pipe with the smouldering tip of his left forefinger. He blew out his forefinger and said, "Yes, please go on."

"Go on? But that's it, that's the whole thing!"

A spot the size of a quarter appeared on Sampson's mauve carpet. It darkened, thickened, grew into a small fruit tree. Sampson picked one of the purple pods, sniffed it, then set it down on his desk. He looked at Lanigan sternly, sadly.

"You've told me about your dream-world before, Tom."

Lanigan nodded.

"We have discussed it, traced its origins, analyzed its meaning for you. In past months we have learned, I believe, why you *need* to cripple yourself with this nightmare fear."

Lanigan nodded unhappily.

"Yet you refuse the insights," Sampson said. "You forget each time that your dream-world is a *dream*, nothing but a dream, operated by arbitrary dream-laws which you have invented to satisfy your psychic needs."

"I wish I could believe that," Lanigan said. "The trouble is my dream-world is so damnably reasonable."

"Not at all," Sampson said. "It is just that your delusion is hermetic, self-enclosed and self-sustaining. A man's actions are based upon certain assumptions about the nature of the world. Grant his assumptions, and his behavior is entirely reasonable. But to change those assumptions, those fundamental axioms, is nearly impossible. For example, how do you prove to a man that he is not being controlled by a secret radio which only he can hear?"

"I see the problem," Lanigan muttered. "And that's me?"

"Yes, Tom. That, in effect, is you. You want me to prove to you that this world is real, and that the world of your dream is false. You propose to give up your fantasy if I supply you with the necessary proofs."

"Yes, exactly!" Lanigan cried.

"But you see, I can't supply them," Sampson said. "The nature of the world is apparent, but unprovable."

Lanigan thought for a while. Then he said, "Look, Doc, I'm not as sick as the guy with the secret radio, am I?"

"No, you're not. You're more reasonable, more rational. You have doubts about the reality of the world; but luckily, you also have doubts about the validity of your delusion."

"Then give it a try," Lanigan said. "I understand your problem; but I swear to you, I'll accept anything I can possibly bring myself to accept."

"It's not my field, really," Sampson said. "This sort of thing calls for a metaphysician. I don't think I'd be very skilled at it. . . ."

"Give it a try," Lanigan pleaded.

"All right, here goes." Sampson's forehead wrinkled and shed as he concentrated. Then he said, "It seems to me that we inspect the world through our senses, and therefore we must in the final analysis accept the testimony of those senses."

Lanigan nodded, and the doctor went on.

"So, we know that a thing exists because our senses tell us it exists. How do we check the accuracy of our observations? By comparing them with the sensory impressions of other men. We know that our senses don't lie when other men's senses agree upon the existence of the thing in question."

Lanigan thought about this, then said, "Therefore, the real world is simply what most men think it is."

Sampson twisted his mouth and said, "I told you that metaphysics was not my forte. Still, I think it is an acceptable demonstration."

"Yes. . . . But Doc, suppose *all* of those observers are wrong? For example, suppose there are many worlds and many realities, not just one? Suppose this is simply

Can You Feel Anything When I Do This? 43

one arbitrary existence out of an infinity of existences? Or suppose that the nature of reality itself is capable of change, and that somehow I am able to perceive that change?"

Sampson sighed, found a little green bat fluttering inside his jacket and absentmindedly crushed it with a ruler.

"There you are," he said. "I can't disprove a single one of your suppositions. I think, Tom, that we had better run through the entire dream."

Lanigan grimaced. "I really would rather not. I have a feeling. . . ."

"I know you do," Sampson said, smiling faintly. "But this will prove or disprove it once and for all, won't it?"

"I guess so," Lanigan said. He took courage—unwisely —and said, "Well, the way it begins, the way my dream starts—"

Even as he spoke the horror came over him. He felt dizzy, sick, terrified. He tried to rise from the couch. The doctor's face ballooned over him. He saw a glint of metal, heard Sampson saying, "Just try to relax . . . brief seizure . . . try to think of something pleasant."

Then either Lanigan or the world or both passed out.

Lanigan and/or the world came back to consciousness. Time may or may not have passed. Anything might or might not have happened. Lanigan sat up and looked at Sampson.

"How do you feel now?" Sampson asked.

"I'm all right," Lanigan said. "What happened?"

"You had a bad moment. Take it easy for a bit."

Lanigan leaned back and tried to calm himself. The doctor was sitting at his desk, writing notes. Lanigan counted to twenty with his eyes closed, then opened them cautiously. Sampson was still writing notes.

Lanigan looked around the room, counted the five pictures on the wall, re-counted them, looked at the green carpet, frowned at it, closed his eyes again. This time he counted to fifty.

"Well, care to talk about it now?" Sampson asked, shutting a notebook.

"No, not just now," Lanigan said. (Five paintings, green carpet.)

"Just as you please," the doctor said. "I think that our time is just about up. But if you'd care to lie down in the anteroom—"

"No, thanks, I'll go home," Lanigan said.

He stood up, walked across the green carpet to the door, looked back at the five paintings and at the doctor, who smiled at him encouragingly. Then Lanigan went through the door and into the anteroom, through the anteroom to the outer door and through that and down the corridor to the stairs and down the stairs to the street.

He walked and looked at the trees, on which green leaves moved faintly and predictably in a faint breeze. There was traffic, which moved soberly down one side of the street and up the other. The sky was an unchanging blue, and had obviously been so for quite some time.

Dream? He pinched himself. A dream pinch? He did not awaken. He shouted. An imaginary shout? He did not waken.

He was in the street of the world of his nightmare.

The street at first seemed like any normal city street. There were paving stones, cars, people, buildings, a sky overhead, a sun in the sky. All perfectly normal. Except that *nothing was happening*.

The pavement never once yielded beneath his feet. Over there was the First National City Bank; it had been here yesterday, which was bad enough; but worse it would be there without fail tomorrow, and the day after that, and the year after that. The First National City Bank (Founded 1892) was grotesquely devoid of possibilities. It would never become a tomb, an airplane, the bones of a prehistoric monster. Sullenly it would remain a building of concrete and steel, madly persisting in its fixity until men with tools came and tediously tore it down.

Lanigan walked through this petrified world, under a blue sky that oozed a sly white around the edges, teasingly promising something that was never delivered. Traffic moved implacably to the right, people crossed at crossings, clocks were within minutes of agreement.

Somewhere between the town lay countryside; but Lanigan knew that the grass did not grow under one's feet; it simply lay still, growing no doubt, but imperceptibly, unusable to the senses. And the mountains were still tall and black, but they were giants stopped in mid-stride. They would never march against a golden (or purple or green) sky.

The essence of life, Dr. Sampson had once said, is change. The essence of death is immobility. Even a corpse has a vestige of life about it as long as its flesh rots, as long as maggots still feast on its blind eye and blowflies suck the juice from the burst intestines.

Lanigan looked around at the corpse of the world and perceived that it was dead.

He screamed. He screamed while people gathered around and looked at him (but didn't do anything or become anything), and then a policeman came as he was supposed to (but the sun didn't change shape once), and then an ambulance came down the invariant street (but without trumpets, minus strumpets, on four wheels instead of a pleasing three or twenty-five) and the ambulance men brought him to a building which was exactly where they expected to find it, and there was a great deal of talk by people who stood untransformed, asking questions in a room with relentlessly white walls.

And there was evening and there was morning, and it was the first day.

GAME: FIRST SCHEMATIC

Perhaps he was not yet fully awake, perhaps that could account for the shock of walking down the dark corridor and through the oval door into the sudden silence and immensity of the arena. The concentric stone tiers rose dizzyingly above his head, stopping down the dome of the sky, concentrating and focusing the heat and energy of the crowd. The morning sun glared off the white sand, and for a moment he couldn't remember where he was.

He looked down at himself: he was wearing a collarless blue shirt and red shorts— A leather mitaxl was strapped to his left hand. In his right hand he held the daenum, its four-foot length heavy and reassuring. He wore padded knee and elbow guards as required by the regulations. He also wore a little feathered yellow cap. The regulations didn't call for it, but they didn't forbid it, either.

All of which was meant to be familiar and reassuring. But was it?

He tested the webbing and linkages of the mitaxl, made sure that the daenum could travel freely on its bronze spindle. He touched his waist and felt the customary soft weight of the sentrae tied to his belt, its rough side turned in. He told himself that everything was in order. But he was uneasy, for it seemed to him—madly enough—that he had never been in an arena before, had never heard of a daenum, didn't even know the name of the game he was supposed to play. But that was crazy, that was nerves, that could be ignored. He shook his head brusquely and took three gliding steps to test the ball-bearings in his skates, reversed and circled his own square.

Can You Feel Anything When I Do This? 47

Now he could hear the crowd, they always got restless just before a contest began; yes, and abusive. It was the skates, of course, the skates were not traditional, the crowd could never forgive him for the skates. But didn't they realize that playing on skates was more difficult than on foot? Did they ever consider the problem of returning a low volley while skating backwards? Didn't they know that the advantage of speed was canceled out by the increased complexities of judgment? Surely they were aware that he could also win on foot!

He rubbed his forehead and looked toward the reviewing stand. The three judges had taken their places, they were looking out through the eye slits in their feathered masks. The blindfolded woman reached into the high wicker basket, selected a ball and threw it to him.

He weighed it in his hand, an oblate sheroid, difficult to serve, harder to return. He saw that his opponent in the opposite court was waiting, knees flexed, body hunched forward. So he threw the ball into the air and quickly, without thinking, put spin on it with the daenum. The crowd became quiet, watching the ball spinning miraculously three feet above the ground. He adjusted tilt with the mitaxl, a routine operation but one that filled him with sudden despair, for he realized that this was not his day to win, not his week, not his year, maybe not his decade . . .

He pulled himself together, let the daenum slide to the end of the spindle, and served. The ball fluttered away from him like a wounded bird, and the crowd roared with laughter. Still, it was a deceptively good stroke, the ball came alive just before entering the net (his patent serve!) and skipped upward and over, catching the opposing player flatfooted.

He turned away, heard the crowd roar again, and knew that his opponent had somehow managed to return it. He saw the ball, heavy with unintentional backspin, come skipping slowly toward him. It was not much of a return; he could have laid into it on rebote, driven his opponent out of position, scored a psychological point. But he chose to let the ball go past him into the backboard; and now, presumably, his opponent had the edge.

He heard a few boos and whistles. He ignored them, it was damned hot today, his legs ached, he was bored. He felt, not for the first time, that the contest had become meaningless. It was ludicrous, when you thought about it—a grown man playing so seriously at a game! After all, life was more than that, life was love and children and sunsets and good food. Why had this contest come to epitomize his entire existence?

Another ball had been put into play, a big, shapeless, mushy thing, too light, not at all his kind of ball. He couldn't get anything into a ball like that. He rejected it, as was his privilege, and rejected the next two as well, out of pique, even though the last one might have been tailord to his talents. But he let it drop away, pivoted on his skates and glided over to the sideline bench. The contest hadn't begun yet, but his right shoulder hurt and he was thirsty.

He drank a cup of water, shading his eyes with the mitaxl, then motioned to the club boy for another cup. He couldn't tell if the judges were watching him or not; presumably they were, he was delaying the match. But it couldn't be helped, he needed time to think out his strategy, for he did like to have a definite game plan. Not a *blueprint* or a *schematic* (despite the advice of several outstanding professionals); just a general strategy, flexible and based upon good general principles and embodying all available information. But of course, he didn't *need* to have a game plan. Like any professional he could play with or without a plan, he could play drunk, sick, or half-dead. He might not win, but he could always play. That was what it meant to be a professional.

He turned now to study the arena, the hatched scoring squares, the black interdicted area, the red and blue striped no-man's land. But suddenly he couldn't remember the rules, couldn't remember how you scored points, didn't know what was fair and what was foul. And, in a panic, he saw himself, a bewildered man dressed in gym clothes, balanced precariously on roller skates, standing in front

Can You Feel Anything When I Do This?

of a hostile crowd, about to play a game he had never before heard of.

He finished his second cup of water and skated back into the court. There was a taste of acid in his mouth, and sweat stung his eyes. The mitaxl creaked as he picked up his stride, and the daenum flopped against his leg like a broken bird.

Here came his ball, shaped like a goddamned *lozenge*, a freak of a ball, an impossible ball even for him, the acknowledged master of impossible balls. He'd never get this one to the net, much less over it!

Of course, if he *did* get it over—

But he'd never get it over.

He told himself without conviction that the game was more important than the win. He hefted the ball, flapped the sentrae into guard position, took up the stylized serving posture. Then he threw the ball down.

The crowd was absolutely quiet.

"Now look," he said, in a conversational voice that carried to the highest sun-drenched bleacher, "I told the management beforehand that I insisted upon a sunscreen. You will note that it has not been forthcoming. Yet, in expectation of it, I did not wear sunglasses. Clearly, this is a breach of contract. Ladies and gentlemen, I am sorry, there will be no game today."

He bowed, sweeping off his feathered cap. There were a few murmurs, a few catcalls, but they took it well, filing out without undue protest. They were used to it, of course: although he was famous for appearing on the courts every day, rain or shine, he didn't actually complete more than a dozen matches a year. He didn't have to, there was plenty of precedent, you could look at the contests-engaged column in any newspaper and see the number of scratches. Even in the Smithsonian where the first historical references to the game were recorded, even there, engraved in stone, you could see that the legendary contenders of antiquity had had spotty attendance records.

Still, he felt bad about it. The judges left and he bowed to them, but they didn't acknowledge his salutation.

He went back to the sidelines and drank another cup of water. When he looked up, he saw that his opponent had left. He glided back into the court and took practice shots against the wall, moving smoothly back and forth across the enameled tiles, retrieving his shots, marveling at his own skill. He was going well now, he was sorry that this one didn't count. But what had the man said? "Everything's easy to hit except the money ball."

At the end of the day the sand was streaked black, and dotted with drops of his sweat and blood. But none of it counted, so he ignored the scattering of applause. He knew that he had practiced in order to stay occupied, and in order to keep his own respect, so that he could continue to believe that he would play and win at this game.

At any rate, he was tired now. He ducked into the dressing room and changed back into street clothes. He went out the back door into the street.

To his surprise it was dark outside. Dark already? What had he been doing all day? Incredibly, he was not completely sure, but it seemed to him that he had been engaging in some kind of weird contest.

He went home then and he wanted to tell his wife about the game, but he couldn't think of what to say or how to tell about it, so he didn't say anything, and when his wife asked how his work had gone, he said all right, by which they both understood that it hadn't gone well, not this time, not today.

DOCTOR ZOMBIE AND HIS
LITTLE FURRY FRIENDS

I think I am fairly safe here. I live at present in a small apartment northeast of the Zócalo, in one of the oldest parts of Mexico City. As a foreigner, my inevitable first impression is how like Spain this country seems, and how different it really is. In Madrid the streets are a maze which draws you continually deeper, toward hidden centers with tedious, well-guarded secrets. Concealment of the commonplace is surely a heritage of the Moors. Whereas Mexican streets are an inverted labyrinth which leads outward toward the mountains, toward openness, toward revelations which remain forever elusive. Nothing is concealed; but nothing in Mexico is comprehensible. This is the way of the Indians, past and present —a defense based upon permeability; a transparent defense like that of the sea anemone.

I find this style profound and compatible. I conform to insight born in Tenochtitlán or Tlaxcala; I conceal nothing, and thus contrive to hide everything.

How often I have envied the thief who has nothing to hide but a handful of game! Some of us are less lucky, some of us possess secrets which won't fit into our pockets, or into our closets; secrets which cannot even be contained in our parlors or buried in our back yards. Gilles de Retz required a private hidden cemetery scarcely smaller than Père La Chaise. My own needs are more modest; but not by much.

I am not a sociable man. I dream of a house in the country, on the barren slopes of Ixtaccíhuatl, where there is no other human habitation for miles in any direction. But that would be madness. The police assume that a man who isolates himself has something to conceal; the equation is as true as it is banal. Those polite, relentless Mexican police! How they distrust foreigners, and how rightfully so! They would have searched my lonely house on some pretext, and the truth would have come out—a three-day sensation for the newspapers.

I have avoided all of that, or at least put it off, by living where I live. Not even García, the most zealous policeman in my neighborhood, can make himself believe that I use this small permeable apartment for *secret ungodly experiments of a terrible nature.* As is rumored.

My door is usually ajar. When the shopkeepers deliver my provisions, I tell them to walk right in. They never do so, they are innately respectful of a man's privacy. But I tell them in any case.

I have three rooms arranged in line. One enters through the kitchen. Next is the parlor, and after that the bedroom. Each room has a door, none of which I ever close completely. Perhaps I carry this fetish of openness too far. For if anyone ever walked through my apartment, pushed the bedroom door fully open and looked inside, I suppose I would have to kill myself.

To date, my callers have never gone beyond the kitchen. I think they are frightened of me.

And why not? I am frightened of myself.

My work forces me into an uncongenial mode of life. I must take all of my meals in my apartment. I am a bad cook; even the meanest neighborhood restaurant exceeds my efforts. Even the sidewalk vendors with their overcooked tacos surpass my indigestible messes.

And to make it worse, I am forced to invent ridiculous reasons for always eating at home. I tell my neighbors that my doctor allows me no spices whatsoever, no chilies, no tomatoes, no salt . . . Why? A rare condition of the liver. How did I contract it? From eating tainted meat many years ago in Jakarta . . .

All of which is easy enough to say, you may think. But I find it difficult to remember the details. A liar is forced to live in a hateful and unnatural state of consistency. His role becomes his punishment.

My neighbors find it easy to accept my contorted explanations. A little incongruity feels very lifelike to them, and they consider themselves excellent arbiters of truth; whereas all they really pass judgment on are questions of verisimilitude.

Still, despite themselves, my neighbors sense something monstrous about me. Eduardo the butcher once said: "Did you know, Doctor, that zombies are allowed no salt? Maybe you are a zombie, eh?"

Where on earth did he learn about zombies? In the cinema, I suppose, or from a comic book. I have seen old women make a sign to avert the evil eye when I pass, and I have heard children whisper behind my back: "Doctor Zombie, Doctor Zombie."

Old women and children! They are the repositories of what little wisdom this race possesses. Yes, and the butchers also know a thing or two.

I am neither a doctor nor a zombie. Nevertheless, the old women and the children are quite right about me. Luckily, no one listens to them.

So I continue to eat in my own kitchen—lamb, kid, pig, rabbit, beef, veal, chicken, and sometimes venison. It is the only way I can get the necessary quantities of meat into my house to feed my animals.

Someone else has recently begun to suspect me. Unfortunately, that man is Diego Juan García, a policeman.

García is stocky, broad-faced, careful, a good cop. Around the Zócalo he is considered incorruptible—an Aztec Cato, but with a better disposition. According to the vegetable woman—who is perhaps in love with me—García believes that I might well be an escaped German war criminal.

It is an amazing conception, factually wrong, but intuitionally correct. García is certain that, somehow, he has hit upon the truth. He would have acted by now if it were not for the intercession of my neighbors. The shoemaker, the butcher, the shoeshine boy, and especially the vegetable woman, all vouch for me. They are bourgeois rationalists, they believe their own projections of my character. They chide García: "Isn't it obvious that this foreigner is a quiet, goodhearted man, a harmless scholar, a dreamer?"

Madly enough, they too are factually wrong, but intuitionally correct.

My invaluable neighbors address me as "Doctor," and sometimes as "Professor." These are honorary degrees which they awarded me quite spontaneously, as a reward to my appearance. I did not solicit a title, but I do not reject it. "Señor Doctor" is another mask behind which I can hide.

I suppose I look to them like a doctor: huge glistening forehead, gray hair bristling from the sides of my balding head, square, stern, wrinkled face. Yes, and my European accent, my careful Spanish constructions, my absent-minded air . . . And my gold-rimmed glasses! What else could I be but a doctor, and a German one at that?

My title demands an occupation, and I claim to be a scholar on extended leave from my university. I tell them that I am writing a book about the Toltecs, a book in which I will collate evidence of a cultural linkage between that mysterious race and the Incas.

"Yes, gentlemen, I expect that my book will create quite a stir in Heidelberg and Bonn. There are vested interests which will be offended. Attempts will doubtless be made to represent me as a crank. My theory, you see, could shake the entire world of pre-Columbian studies . . ."

I had prepared the above personality before coming to Mexico. I read Stephens, Prescott, Vaillant, Alfonso Caso. I even went to the trouble of copying out the first third of Dreyer's discredited thesis on cultural diffusion, in which he postulates a Mayan-Toltec cultural exchange. That gave me an opus of some eighty handwritten pages which I could claim as my own. The unfinished manuscript was my excuse for being in Mexico. Anyone could glance at the erudite pages scattered over my desk and see for himself what sort of man I was.

I thought that would suffice; but I hadn't allowed for the dynamism inherent in my role. Señor Ortega, my grocer, is also interested in pre-Columbian studies, and is disturbingly knowledgeable. Señor Andrade, the barber, was born in a pueblo within five miles of the ruins of Teotihuacán. And little Jorge Silverio, the shoeshine boy whose mother works in a *tortillería,* dreams of attending a great university, and asks me very humbly if I might use my influence at Bonn . . .

I am the victim of my neighbors' expectations. I have become *their* professor, not mine. Because of them I must spend endless hours at the National Museum of Anthropology, and waste whole days at Teotihuacán, Tula, Xochicalco. My neighbors force me to work hard at my scholarly pursuit. And I have become quite literally what I purported to be: an expert, possessed of formidable knowledge, more than a little mad.

The role has penetrated me, mingled with me, transformed me; to the extent that now I really *do* believe in the likelihood of a Toltec-Incan connection, I have unassailable evidence, I have seriously considered publishing my findings . . .

All of which I find tiresome and quite beside the point.

I had a bad scare last month. My landlady, Señora Elvira Macias, stopped me on the street and demanded that I get rid of my dog.

"But, señora, I have no dog."

"Excuse me, señor, but you do have a dog. I heard it last night, whining and scratching at your door. And my rules, which were also those of my poor late husband, expressly forbid—"

"My dear señora, you must be mistaken. I can assure you..."

And there was García, inevitable as death, in freshly starched khakis, puffing on a Delicado and listening to our conversation.

"A scratching sound? Perhaps it was the termites, señora, or the cockroaches."

She shook her head. "It was not that kind of sound."

"Rats, then. Your building, I regret to say, is infested with rats."

"I know very well what rats sound like," Señora Elvira said, invincibly ingenuous. "But this was not like that, this was a doglike sound which came from your apartment. And as I have told you, I have an absolute rule against pets."

García was watching me, and I saw reflected in his eyes my deeds at Dachau, Bergen-Belsen, Theresienstadt. I wanted to tell him that he was wrong, that I was one of the victims, that I had spent the war years as a prisoner in the Tjilatjap concentration camp in Java.

But I also knew that the specific facts did not matter. My crimes against humanity were real enough: García just happened to be sensing next year's frightfulness rather than last year's.

I might have confessed everything at that moment if Señora Elvira had not turned to García and said, "Well, what are you going to do about all this? He keeps a dog, perhaps two dogs, he keeps God knows what in that apartment of his. What are you going to do?"

García said nothing. His immobile face reminded me of the stone mask of Tlaloc in the Cholula museum. My own reaction was in keeping with that transparent defense by which I hide my secrets. I ground my teeth, flared my nostrils, tried to simulate the *furia español*.

"Dogs?" I howled. "I'll show you dogs! Come up and search my apartment! I will pay you a hundred pesos for each dog you find, two hundred for purebreeds. You come too, García, and bring all your friends. Perhaps I have a horse up there as well, eh? And maybe a pig?

Can You Feel Anything When I Do This? 57

Bring witnesses, bring newspaper reporters, I want my menagerie to be noted with accuracy."

"Calm yourself," García said, unimpressed by my rage.

"I will calm myself after we dispose of the dogs!" I shouted. "Come, señora, enter my rooms and look under the bed for your hallucinations. And when you are satisfied, you will kindly refund me the remainder of my month's rent and my month's security, and I will go live somewhere else with my invisible dogs."

García looked at me curiously. I suppose he has seen a great deal of bravado in his time. It is said to be typical of a certain type of criminal. He said to Señora Elvira: "Shall we take a look?"

My landlady surprised me. She said—incredibly!— "Certainly not! The gentleman has given his word." And she turned and walked away.

I was about to complete the bluff by insisting that García search for himself if he were not completely satisfied. Luckily, I stopped myself. García is no respector of properties. He is not afraid of making a fool of himself.

"I am tired," I said. "I am going to lie down."

And that was the end of it.

This time I locked my front door. It had been a near thing. While we had been talking, the poor wretched creature had gnawed through its leash and died on the kitchen floor.

I disposed of it in the usual way, by feeding it to the others. Thereafter I doubled my precautions. I bought a radio to cover what little noise they made. I put heavy straw matting under their cages. And I masked their odor with heavy tobacco, for I thought that incense would be too obvious.

But it is strange and ironic that anyone should suspect *me* of keeping dogs. They are my implacable enemies. They know what goes on in my apartment. They have allied themselves with mankind. They are renegade animals, just as I am a renegade human. If the dogs could speak, they would hurry to the police station with their *denunciamentos*.

When the battle against humanity is finally begun, the dogs will have to stand or fall with their masters.

A note of cautious optimism: the last litter was quite promising. Four of the twelve survived, and grew sleek and clever and strong. But they are not as ferocious as I had expected. That part of their genetic inheritance seems to have been lost. They actually seem fond of me—like dogs! But this surely can be bred out of them.

Mankind has dire legends of hybrids produced by the cross-breeding of various species. Among these are the chimera, the griffin, and the sphinx, to name but a few. It seems to me that these antique nightmares might have been a *memory of the future*—like García's perception of my not-yet-committed crimes.

Pliny and Diodorus record the monstrous offspring of camel and ostrich, lion and eagle, horse, dragon, and tiger. What would they have thought of a composite wolverine and rat? What would a modern biologist think of this prodigy?

The scientists of today will deny its existence even when my heraldic beasts are swarming into towns and cities. No reasonable man will believe in a creature the size of wolf, as savage and cunning as a wolverine, as social, adaptable, and as great a breeder as a rat. A confirmed rationalist will deny credence to this indescribable and apocryphal beast even as it tears out his throat.

And he will be almost right in his skepticism. Such a product of cross-hybridization was clearly impossible—until I produced it last year.

Secrecy can begin as a necessity and end as a habit. Even in this journal, in which I intended to tell everything,

I see that I have not recorded my reasons for breeding monsters, nor what I intend them to do.

Their work should begin in about three months, in early July. By then, local residents will be remarking on a horde of animals which has begun to infest the slums surrounding the Zócalo. Descriptions will be hazy, but people will remark on the size of these creatures, their ferocity and elusiveness. The authorities will be notified, the newspapers will take note. The blame will probably be laid to wolves or wild dogs at first, despite the uncanine appearance of these beasts.

Standard methods of extermination will be tried, and will fail. The mysterious creatures will spread out through the capital, and then into the wealthy suburbs of Pedregal and Coyoacán. It will be known by now that they are omnivores, like man himself. And it will be suspected—correctly—that they possess an extremely high rate of reproduction.

Perhaps not until later will their high degree of intelligence be appreciated.

The armed forces will be called in, to no avail. The air force will thunder over the countryside; but what will they find to bomb? These creatures present no mass target for conventional weaponry. They live behind the walls, under the sofa, inside the closet—always just beyond the outer edge of your eyesight.

Poison? But these hybrids eat what you possess, not what you offer.

And besides, it is August now, the situation is completely out of hand. The army is spread symbolically throughout Mexico City; but the cohorts of the beasts have overrun Toluca, Ixtapan, Tepalcingo, Cuernavaca, and they have been reported in San Luis Potosí, in Oaxaca and Veracruz.

Scientists confer, crash programs are drawn up, experts come to Mexico from all over the world. The beasts hold no conferences and publish no manifestos. They simply spawn and spread, north to Durango, south to Villahermosa.

The United States closes its borders; another symbolic gesture. The beasts come down to Piedras Negras, they cross the Eagle Pass without permission; unauthorized they appear in El Paso, Laredo, Brownsville.

They sweep across the plains and deserts like a whirlwind, they flow into the cities like a tidal wave. Doctor Zombie's little furry friends have arrived, and they are here to stay.

And at last mankind realizes that the problem is not how to exterminate these creatures. No, the problem is how to prevent these creatures from exterminating man.

This can be done, I have no doubt. But it is going to require the full efforts and ingenuity of the human race.

That is what I expect to achieve by breeding monsters.

You see, something must be done. I intend my hybrids to act as a counterbalance, a load to control the free-running human engine that is tearing up the earth and itself. I consider this job ethically imperative. After all: Does man have the right to exterminate whatever species he pleases? Must everything in creation serve his ill-considered schemes, or be obliterated? Don't all life forms and systems have a right to live, an absolute right with no possibility of qualification?

Despite the extremity of the measure, there will be benefits to mankind. No one will have to worry again about hydrogen bombs, germ warfare, defoliation, pollution, greenhouse effect, and the like. Overnight, these preoccupations will become—medieval. Man will return to a life in nature. He will still be unique, still intelligent, still a predator; but now he will be subject again to certain checks and balances which he had previously evaded.

His most prized freedom will remain; he will still be at liberty to kill; he will simply lose the ability to exterminate.

Pneumonia is a great leveler of aspirations. It has killed my creatures. Yesterday the last of them raised its head and looked at me. Its large pale eyes were filmed over.

It raised a paw, extended its claws, and scratched me lightly on the forearm.

I cried then, for I knew that my poor beast had done that only to please me, knowing how much I desired it to be fierce, implacable, a scourge against mankind.

The effort was too much. Those marvelous eyes closed. It died with barely a twitch.

Pneumonia is not really a sufficient explanation, of course. Beyond that, the will was simply not there. No species has had much vitality since man pre-empted the earth. The slave-raccoons still play in the tattered Adirondack forests, and the slave-lions sniff beer cans in Kruger Park. They and all the others exist only on our sufferance, as squatters on our land. And they know it.

Under the circumstances, you can't expect to find much vitality and spirit among non-humans. Spirit is the property of the victors.

The death of my last beast has become my own end. I am too tired and too heartsick to begin again. I regret that I have failed mankind. I regret having failed the lions, ostriches, tigers, whales, and other species threatened with extinction. But most of all I regret having failed the sparrows, crows, rats, hyenas—the vermin of the earth, the trash species who exist only to be exterminated by man. My truest sympathy has always been with the outlawed, abandoned, or worthless, in whose categories I include myself.

Are they vermin simply because they do not serve man? Don't all life forms and systems have a right to live, an absolute right with no possibility of qualification? Must everything in creation continue to serve one species, or be obliterated?

Some other man must feel as I do. I ask him to take up the fight, become a guerrilla against his own kind, oppose them as he would oppose a raging fire.

This record has been written for that hypothetical man.

As for me: not long ago, García and another official came to my apartment on a "routine" health inspection.

They found the bodies of several of my composite creatures, which I had not yet had the opportunity to destroy. I was arrested and charged with cruelty to animals, and with operating a slaughter-house without license.

I shall plead guilty to the charges. Despite their falseness, I recognize them as essentially and undeniably true.

THE CRUEL EQUATIONS

After landing on Regulus V, the men of the Yarmolinsky Expedition made camp and activated PR–22–0134, their perimeter robot, whom they called Max. The robot was a voice-activated, bipedal mechanism whose function was to guard the camp against the depredations of aliens, in the event that aliens were ever encountered. Max had originally been a regulation gunmetal gray, but on the interminable outward trip they had repainted him a baby blue. Max stood exactly four feet high. The men of the expedition had come to think of him as a kindly, reasonable little metal man—a ferrous gnome, a miniature Tin Woodman of Oz.

They were wrong, of course. Their robot had none of the qualities which they projected onto him. PR–22–0134 was no more reasonable than a McCormick harvester, no more kindly than an automated steel mill. Morally, he might be compared to a turbine or a radio, but not to anything human. PR–22–0134's only human attribute was potentiality.

Little Max, baby blue with red eyes, circled the perimeter of the camp, his sensors alert. Captain Beatty and Lieutenant James took off in the hoverjet for a week of exploration. They left Lieutenant Halloran to mind the store.

Halloran was a short, stocky man with a barrel chest and bandy legs. He was cheerful, freckled, tough, profane, and resourceful. He ate lunch and acknowledged a radio check from the exploring team. Then he unfolded a canvas chair and sat back to enjoy the scenery.

Regulus V was a pretty nice place, if you happened to be an admirer of desolation. A superheated landscape of rock, gravel, and lava stretched on all sides. There were some birds that looked like sparrows and some animals that looked like coyotes. A few cacti scratched out a bare living.

Halloran pulled himself to his feet. "Max! I'm going to take a look outside the perimeter. You'll be in charge while I'm gone."

The robot stopped patrolling. "Yes sir, I will be in charge."

"You will not allow any aliens to come busting in; especially the two-headed kind with their feet on backwards."

"Very well, sir." Max had no sense of humor when it came to aliens. "Do you have the password, Mr. Halloran?"

"I got it, Max. How about you?"

"I have it, sir."

"OK. See you later." Halloran left the camp.

After examining the real estate for an hour and finding nothing of interest, Halloran came back. He was pleased to see PR–22–0134 patrolling along the perimeter. It meant that everything was all right.

"Hi there, Max," he called. "Any messages for me?"

"Halt," the robot said. "Give the password."

"Cut the comedy, Max. I'm in no mood for—"

"Halt!" the robot shouted, as Halloran was about to cross the perimeter.

Halloran came to an abrupt stop. Max's photoelectric eyes had flared, and a soft double click announced that his primary armament was activated. Halloran decided to proceed with caution.

"I am halted. My name is Halloran. OK now, Maxie?"

"Give the password, please."

" 'Bluebells,' " Halloran said. "Now, if you don't mind—"

"Do not cross the perimeter," the robot said. "Your password is incorrect."

"The hell it is. I gave it to you myself."

Can You Feel Anything When I Do This? 65

"That was the previous password."

"Previous? You're out of your semi-solid mind," Halloran said. " 'Bluebells' is the only password, and you didn't get any new one because there isn't any new one. Unless . . ."

The robot waited— Halloran considered the unpleasant thought from various angles, and at last put words to it.

"Unless Captain Beatty gave you a new password before he left. Is *that* what happened?"

"Yes," the robot said.

"I should have thought of it," Halloran said. He grinned, but he was annoyed. There had been slipups like this before. But there had always been someone inside the camp to correct them.

Still, there was nothing to worry about. When you came right down to it, the situation was more than a little funny. And it could be resolved with just a modicum of reason.

Halloran was assuming, of course, that PR robots possess a modicum of reason.

"Max," Halloran said, "I see how it probably happened. Captain Beatty probably gave you a new password. But he failed to tell me about it. I then compounded his error by neglecting to check on the password situation before I left the perimeter."

The robot made no comment. Halloran went on. "The mistake, in any case, is easily corrected."

"I sincerely hope so," the robot said.

"Of course it is," Halloran said, a little less confidently. "The captain and I follow a set procedure in these matters. When he gives you a password, he also transmits it to me orally. But, just in case there is any lapse—like now—he also writes it down."

"Does he?" the robot asked.

"Yes, he does," Halloran said. "Always. Invariably. Which includes this time too, I hope. Do you see that tent behind you?"

The robot swiveled one sensor, keeping the other fixed on Halloran. "I see it."

"OK. Inside the tent, there is a table. On the table is a gray metal clipboard."

"Correct," Max said.

"Fine! Now then, there is a sheet of paper in the clipboard. On it is a list of vital data—emergency radio frequencies, that sort of thing. On the top of the paper, circled in red, is the current password."

The robot extended and focused his sensor, then retracted it. He said to Halloran, "What you say is true, but irrelevant. I am concerned only with your knowledge of the actual password, not its location. If you can state the password, I must let you into the camp. If not, I must keep you out."

"This is insane!" Halloran shouted. "Max, you legalistic idiot, it's *me*, Halloran, and you damned well know it! We've been together since the day you were activated! Now will you please stop playing Horatio at the bridge and let me in?"

"Your resemblance to Mr. Halloran *is* uncanny," the robot admitted. "But I am neither equipped nor empowered to conduct identity tests; nor am I permitted to act on the basis of my perceptions. The only proof I can accept is the password itself."

Halloran fought down his rage. In a conversational tone he said, "Max, old buddy, it sounds like you're implying that I'm an alien."

"Since you do not have the password," Max said, "I must proceed on that assumption."

"Max!" Halloran shouted, stepping forward, "for Christ's sake!"

"Do not approach the perimeter!" the robot said, his sensors flaring. "Whoever or whatever you are, stand back!"

"All right, I'm standing back," Halloran said quickly. "Don't get so nervous."

He backed away from the perimeter and waited until the robot's sensors had gone quiescent. Then he sat down on a rock. He had some serious thinking to do.

Can You Feel Anything When I Do This? 67

It was almost noon in Regulus's thousand-hour day. The twin suns hung overhead, distorted white blobs in a dead white sky. They moved sluggishly above a dark granite landscape, slow-motion juggernauts who destroyed what they touched.

An occasional bird soared in weary circles through the dry fiery air. A few small animals crept from shadow to shadow. A creature that looked like a wolverine gnawed at a tent peg, and was ignored by a small blue robot. A man sat on a rock and watched the robot.

Halloran, already feeling the effects of exposure and thirst, was trying to understand his situation and to plan a way out of it.

He wanted water. Soon he would need water. Not long after that, he would die for lack of water.

There was no known source of potable water within walking distance, except in the camp.

There was plenty of water in the camp. But he couldn't get to it past the robot.

Beatty and James would routinely try to contact him in three days, but they would probably not be alarmed if he didn't reply. Short-wave reception was erratic, even on Earth. They would try again in the evening and again the next day. Failing to raise him then, they would come back.

Call it four Earth days, then. How long could he go without water?

The answer depended on his rate of water loss. When he had sustained a total liquid loss of between ten and fifteen percent of his body weight, he would go into shock. This could happen with disastrous suddenness. Bedouin tribesmen, separated from their supplies, had been known to succumb in twenty-four hours. Stranded motorists in the American Southwest, trying to walk out of the Baker or Mojave Deserts, sometimes didn't last out the day.

Regulus V was as hot as the Kalahari, and had less humidity than Death Valley. A day on Regulus stretched for just under a thousand Earth hours. It was noon, he had five hundred hours of unremitting sunshine ahead of him without shelter or shade.

How long could he last? One earth day. Two, at the most optimistic estimate.

Forget about Beatty and James. He had to get water from the camp, and he had to get it fast.

That meant he had to find a way past the robot.

He decided to try logic. "Max, you must know that I, Halloran, left the camp and that I, Halloran, returned an hour later, and that it is I, Halloran, now standing in front of you without the password."

"The probabilities are very strongly in favor of your interpretation," the robot admitted.

"Well, then—"

"But I cannot act on probabilities, or even near-certainties. After all, I have been created for the express purpose of dealing with aliens, despite the extremely low probability that I will ever meet one."

"Can you at least give me a canteen of water?"

"No. That would be against orders."

"When did you ever get orders about giving out water?"

"I didn't, not specifically. But the conclusion flows from my primary directive. I am not supposed to aid or assist aliens."

Halloran then said a great many things, very rapidly and in a loud voice. His statements were pungently and idiomatically Terran; but Max ignored them since they were abusive, tendentious, and entirely without merit.

After a while, the alien who called himself Halloran moved out of sight behind a pile of rocks.

After some minutes, a creature sauntered out from behind a pile of rocks, whistling.

"Hello there, Max," the creature said.

"Hello, Mr. Halloran," the robot replied.

Halloran stopped ten feet away from the perimeter. "Well," he said, "I've been looking around, but there's

Can You Feel Anything When I Do This?

not much to see. Anything happen here while I've been gone?"

"Yes, sir," Max said. "An alien tried to enter the camp."

Halloran raised both eyebrows. "Is that a fact?"

"Indeed it is, sir."

"What did this alien look like?"

"He looked very much like you, Mr. Halloran."

"God in heaven!" Halloran exclaimed. "How did you know he was *not* me?"

"Because he tried to enter the camp without giving the password. That, of course, the real Mr. Halloran would never do."

"Exactly so," Halloran said. "Good work, Maxie. We'll have to keep our eyes open for that fellow."

"Yes, sir. Thank you, sir."

Halloran nodded casually. He was pleased with himself. He had figured out that Max, by the very terms of his construction, would have to deal with each encounter as unique, and to dispose of it according to its immediate merits. This had to be so, since Max was not permitted to reason on the basis of prior experiences.

Max had built-in biases. He assumed that Earthmen always have the password. He assumed that aliens never have the password, but always try to enter the camp. Therefore, a creature who did not try to enter the camp must be presumed to be free of the alien camp-entering compulsion, and therefore to be an Earthman, until proven otherwise.

Halloran thought that was pretty good reasoning for a man who had lost several percent of his body fluids. Now he had to hope that the rest of his plan would work as well.

"Max," he said, "during my inspection, I made one rather disturbing discovery."

"Sir?"

"I found that we are camped on the edge of a fault in this planet's crust. The lines of the schism are unmistakable; they make the San Andreas Fault look like a hairline fracture."

"Sounds bad, sir. Is there much risk?"

"You bet your tin ass there's much risk. And much risk means much work. You and I, Maxie, are going to shift the entire camp about two miles due west. Immediately! So pick up the canteens and follow me."

"Yes, sir," Max said. "As soon as you release me."

"OK, I release you," Halloran said. "Hurry up!"

"I can't," the robot said. "You must release me by giving the current password and stating that it is canceled. Then I'll be able to stop guarding this particular perimeter."

"There's no time for formalities," Halloran said tightly. "The new password is 'whitefish.' Get moving, Max, I just felt a tremor."

"I didn't feel anything."

"Why should you?" Halloran snapped. "You're just a PR robot, not an Earthman with special training and finely attuned sensory apparatus. Damn, there it goes again! You must have felt it that time!"

"I think I did feel it!"

"Then get moving!"

"Mr. Halloran, I can't! It is physically impossible for me to leave this perimeter without a formal release! Please, sir, release me!"

"Don't get so excited," Halloran said. "On second thought, we're going to leave the camp right here."

"But the earthquake—"

"I've just made a new calculation. We've got more time than I had thought. I'm going to take another look around."

Halloran moved behind the rocks, out of the robot's sight. His heart was beating heavily, and the blood in his veins felt thick and sluggish. Bright spots were dancing before his eyes. He diagnosed an incipient sunstroke, and forced himself to sit very quietly in a patch of shade.

The endless day stretched on. The amorphous white blob of the double suns crept an inch toward the horizon. PR–22–0134 guarded his perimeter.

A breeze sprang up, turned into half a gale, and blew sand against Max's unblinking sensors. The robot trudged

Can You Feel Anything When I Do This? 71

on, keeping to an exact circle. The wind died down and a figure appeared among the rocks some twenty yards away. Someone was watching him: was it Halloran, or the alien? Max refused to speculate. He guarded his perimeter.

A small creature like a coyote darted out of the desert and ran a zigzag course almost under Max's feet. A large bird dived down in pursuit. There was a thin, high scream and blood was splashed against one of the tents. The bird flapped heavily into the air with something writhing in its claws.

Max paid no attention to this. He was watching a humanoid creature stagger toward him out of the rocks.

The creature stopped. "Good day, Mr. Halloran," Max said at once. "I feel that I should mention, sir, that you show definite signs of dehydration. That is a condition which leads to shock, unconsciousness, and death, unless attended to promptly."

"Shut up," Halloran said, in a husky, heat-parched voice.

"Very well, Mr. Halloran."

"And stop calling me Mr. Halloran."

"Why should I do that, sir?"

"Because I am not Halloran. I am an alien."

"Indeed?" the robot said.

"Yes, indeed. Do you doubt my word?"

"Well, your mere unsupported statement—"

"Never mind, I'll give you proof. *I do not know the password*. Is that proof enough?"

When the robot still hesitated, Halloran said, "Look, Mr. Halloran told me that I should remind you of your own fundamental definitions, which are the criteria by which you perform your job. To wit: an earthman is a sentient creature who knows the password; an alien is a sentient creature who does not know the password."

"Yes," the robot said reluctantly, "knowledge of the password is my yardstick. But still, I sense something wrong. Suppose you're lying to me?"

"If I'm lying, then I must be an Earthman who knows there's no danger. But you know that I'm not lying because you know that no Earthman would lie about the password."

"I don't know if I can assume that."

"You must. No Earthman wants to appear as an alien, does he?"

"Of course not."

"And a password is the only certain differentiation between a human and an alien?"

"Yes."

"Then the case is proven."

"I'm still not sure," Max said, and Halloran realized that the robot was reluctant to receive instruction from an alien, even if the alien was only trying to prove that he was an alien.

He waited. After a while, Max said, "All right, I agree that you are an alien. Accordingly, I refuse to let you into the camp."

"I'm not asking you to let me in. The point is, I am Halloran's prisoner, and you know what that means."

The robot blinked his sensors rapidly. "I don't know what that means."

"It means," Halloran said, "that you must follow Halloran's orders concerning me. His orders are that I must be detained within the perimeter of the camp, and must not be released unless he gives specific orders to that effect."

Max cried, "Mr. Halloran knows that I can't let you into the camp!"

"Of course! But Halloran is telling you to *imprison* me in the camp, which is an entirely different matter."

"Is it, really?"

"It certainly is! You must know that Earthmen *always* imprison aliens who try to break into their camp!"

"I seem to have heard something to that effect," Max said. "Still, I cannot allow you in. But I can guard you here, just in front of the camp."

"That's not very good," Halloran said sulkily.

"I'm sorry, but it's the best I can do."

"Oh, very well," Halloran said, sitting down on the sand. "I am your prisoner, then."

"Yes."

Can You Feel Anything When I Do This? 73

"Then give me a drink of water."

"I am not allowed—"

"Damn it, you certainly know that alien prisoners are to be treated with the courtesy appropriate to their rank and are to be given the necessities of life according to the Geneva Convention and other international protocols."

"Yes, I've heard about that," Max said. "What is your rank?"

"Jamisdar, senior grade. My serial number is 12278031. And I need water immediately, because I'll die without it."

Max thought for several seconds. At last he said, "I will give you water. But only after Mr. Halloran has had water."

"Surely there's enough for both of us?" Halloran asked, trying to smile in a winning manner.

"That," Max said firmly, "is for Mr. Halloran to decide."

"All right," Halloran said, getting to his feet.

"Wait! Stop! Where are you going?"

"Just behind those rocks," Halloran said. "It's time for my noon prayer, which I must do in utter privacy."

"But what if you escape?"

"What would be the use?" Halloran asked, walking off. "Halloran would simply capture me again."

"True, true, the man's a genius," the robot muttered.

Very little time passed. Suddenly, Halloran came out of the rocks.

"Mr Halloran?" Max asked.

"That's me," Halloran said cherfully. "Did my prisoner get here OK?"

"Yes, sir. He's over there in the rocks, praying."

"No harm in that," Halloran said. "Listen, Max, when he comes out again, make sure he gets some water."

"I'll be glad to. After you have had your water, sir."

"Hell, I'm not even thirsty. Just see that the poor damned alien gets some."

"I can't, not until I've seen you drink your fill. The

state of dehydration I mentioned, sir, is now more advanced. You are not far from collapse. I insist and I implore you—drink!"

"All right, stop nagging, get me a canteen."

"Oh, sir!"

"Eh? What's the matter?"

"You know I can't leave my post here on the perimeter."

"Why in hell can't you?"

"It's against orders. And also, because there's an alien behind those rocks."

"I'll keep watch for you, Max old boy, and you fetch a canteen like a good boy."

"It's good of you to offer, sir, but I can't allow that. I am a PR robot, constructed for the sole purpose of guarding the camp. I must not turn that responsibility over to anyone else, not even an Earthman or another PR robot, until the password is given and I am relieved of duty."

"Yeah, yeah," Halloran muttered. "Any place I start, it still comes out zero." Painfully he dragged himself behind the rocks.

"What's the matter?" the robot asked. "What did I say?"

There was no answer.

"Mr. Halloran? Jamisdar Alien?"

Still no answer. Max continued to guard his perimeter.

Halloran was tired. His throat hurt from talking with a stupid robot, and his body hurt all over from the endless blows of the double sun. He had gone beyond sunburn; he was blackened, crusted over, a roast turkey of a man. Pain, thirst, and fatigue dominated him, leaving no room for any emotion except anger.

He was furious at himself for being caught in so absurd a situation, for letting himself be killed so casually. ("Halloran? Oh, yes, he didn't know the password, poor devil, and he died of exposure not fifty yards from water and shelter. Sad, strange, funny sort of end . . .")

It was anger that kept him going now, that enabled

Can You Feel Anything When I Do This? 75

him to review his situation and to search for a way into the camp.

He had convinced the robot that he was an Earthman. Then he had convinced the robot that he was an alien. Both approaches had failed when it came to the crucial issue of entry into the camp.

What was there left to try now?

He rolled over and stared up into the glowing white sky. Black specks moved across his line of vision. Hallucination? No, birds were circling. They were ignoring their usual diet of coyotes, waiting for the collapse of something really tasty, a walking banquet...

Halloran forced himself to sit upright. Now, he told himself, I must review the situation and search for a loophole.

From Max's viewpoint, all sentient creatures who possess the password are Earthmen; all sentient creatures who do not possess the password are aliens.

Which means...

Means what? For a second, Halloran thought he had stumbled on to the key to the puzzle. But he was having difficulty concentrating. The birds were circling lower. One of the coyotes had come out and was sniffing at his shoes.

Forget all that. Concentrate. Become a practical automatologist.

Really, when you get right down to it, Max is *stupid*. He wasn't designed to detect frauds, except in the most limited capacity. His criteria are—archaic. Like that story about how Plato defined man as a featherless biped, and Diogenes the Cynic produced a plucked chicken which he maintained fitted the definition. Plato thereupon changed his definition to state that man was a featherless biped with broad nails.

But what has that got to do with Max?

Halloran shook his head savagely, trying to force himself to concentrate. But all he could see was Plato's man —a six-foot chicken without a feather on his body, but with broad fingernails.

Max was vulnerable. He had to be! Unlike Plato, he

couldn't change his mind. Max was stuck with his definitions, and with their logical consequences . . .

"Well, I'll be damned," Halloran said. "I do believe I have figured a way."

He tried to think it through, but found he wasn't able. He simply had to try it, and win or lose on the result. "Max," he said softly, "one plucked chicken is coming up. Or rather, one unplucked chicken. Put *that* in your cosmology and smoke it!"

He wasn't sure what he meant, but he knew what he was going to do.

Captain Beatty and Lieutenant James returned to the camp at the end of three Earth days. They found Halloran unconscious and delirious, a victim of dehydration and sunstroke. He raved about how Plato had tried to keep him out of the camp, and how Halloran had transformed himself into a six-foot chicken without broad fingernails, thus getting the best of the learned philosopher and his robot buddy.

Max had given him water, wrapped his body in wet blankets, and had produced black shade out of a double sheet of plastic. Halloran would recover in a day or two.

He had written a note before passing out: *No password couldn't get back in tell factory install emergency bypass in PR robots.*

Beatty couldn't make any sense out of Halloran, so he questioned Max. He heard about Halloran's trip of inspection and the various aliens who looked exactly like him, and what they said and what Halloran said. Obviously, these were all increasingly desperate attempts on Halloran's part to get back into the camp.

"But what happened after that?" Beatty asked. "How did he finally get in?"

"He didn't 'get in,' " Max said. "He simply *was* in at one point."

"But how did he get past you?"

"He didn't! That would have been quite impossible. Mr. Halloran simply *was* inside the camp."

Can You Feel Anything When I Do This? 77

"I don't understand," Beatty said.

"Quite frankly, sir, I don't either. I'm afraid that only Mr. Halloran can answer your question."

"It'll be awhile before Halloran talks to anyone," Beatty said. "Still, if he figured out a way, I suppose I can, too."

Beatty and James both tried, but they couldn't come up with the answer. They weren't desperate enough or angry enough, and they weren't even thinking along the right lines. To understand how Halloran had gotten in, it was necessary to view the final course of events from Max's viewpoint.

Heat, wind, birds, rock, suns, I disregard the irrelevant. I guard the camp perimeter against aliens.

Now something is coming toward me, out of the rocks, out of the desert. It is a large creature, it has hair hanging over its face, it creeps on four limbs.

I challenge. It snarls at me. I challenge again, in a more pre-emptory manner, I switch on my armament, I threaten. The creature growls and keeps on crawling toward the camp.

I consult my definitions in order to produce an appropriate response.

I know that humans and aliens are both classes of sentient creature characterized by intelligence, which is expressed through the faculty of speech. This faculty is invariably employed to respond to my challenges.

Humans always answer correctly when asked the password.

Aliens always answer incorrectly when asked the password.

Both aliens and humans always answer—correctly or incorrectly—when asked the password.

Since this is invariably so, I must assume that any creature which does *not* answer my challenge is *unable* to answer, and can be ignored.

Birds and reptiles can be ignored. This large beast which crawls past me can also be ignored. I pay no attention to the creature; but I keep my sensors at extended alert, because Mr. Halloran is somewhere out in the desert. There is also an alien out there, a Jamisdar.

But what is this? It is Mr. Halloran, miraculously back in the camp, groaning, suffering from dehydration and sunstroke. The beast who crept past me is gone without trace, and the Jamisdar is presumably still praying in the rocks . . .

THE SAME TO YOU DOUBLED

In New York, it never fails, the doorbell rings just when you've plopped down onto the couch for a well-deserved snooze. Now, a person of character would say, "To hell with that, a man's home is his castle and they can slide any telegrams under the door." But if you're like Edelstein, not particularly strong on character, then you think to yourself that maybe it's the blonde from 12C who has come up to borrow a jar of chili powder. Or it would even be some crazy film producer who wants to make a movie based on the letters you've been sending your mother in Santa Monica. (And why not; don't they make movies out of worse material than that?)

Yet this time, Edelstein had really decided not to answer the bell. Lying on the couch, his eyes still closed, he called out, "I don't want any."

"Yes you do," a voice from the other side of the door replied.

"I've got all the encyclopedias, brushes and waterless cookery I need," Edelstein called back wearily. "Whatever you've got, I've got it already."

"Look," the voice said, "I'm not selling anything. I want to give you something."

Edelstein smiled the thin, sour smile of the New Yorker who knows that if someone made him a gift of a package of genuine, unmarked $20 bills, he'd still somehow end up having to pay for it.

"If it's *free*," Edelstein answered, "then I *definitely* can't afford it."

"But I mean *really* free," the voice said. "I mean free that it won't cost you anything now or ever."

"I'm not interested," Edelstein replied, admiring his firmness of character.

The voice did not answer.

Edelstein called out, "Hey, if you're still there, please go away."

"My dear Mr. Edelstein," the voice said, "cynicism is merely a form of naïveté. Mr. Edelstein, wisdom is discrimination."

"He gives me lectures now," Edelstein said to the wall.

"All right," the voice said, "forget the whole thing, keep your cynicism and your racial prejudice; do I need this kind of trouble?"

"Just a minute," Edelstein answered. "What makes you think I'm prejudiced?"

"Let's not crap around," the voice said. "If I was raising funds for Hadassah or selling Israel bonds, it would have been different. But, obviously, I am what I am, so excuse me for living."

"Not so fast," Edelstein said. "As far as I'm concerned, you're just a voice from the other side of the door. For all I know, you could be Catholic or Seventh-Day Adventist or even Jewish."

"*You knew*," the voice responded.

"Mister, I swear to you—"

"Look," the voice said, "it doesn't matter, I come up against a lot of this kind of thing. Goodbye, Mr. Edelstein."

"Just a minute," Edelstein replied.

He cursed himself for a fool. How often had he fallen for some huckster's line, ending up, for example, paying $9.98 for an illustrated two-volume *Sexual History of Mankind*, which his friend Manowitz had pointed out he could have bought in any Marboro bookstore for $2.98?

But the voice was right. Edelstein had somehow known that he was dealing with a goy.

And the voice would go away thinking, *The Jews, they think they're better than anyone else*. Further, he would tell this to his bigoted friends at the next meeting of the

Can You Feel Anything When I Do This? 81

Elks or the Knights of Columbus, and there it would be, another black eye for the Jews.

"I do have a weak character," Edelstein thought sadly.

He called out, "All right! You can come in! But I warn you from the start, I am not going to buy anything."

He pulled himself to his feet and started toward the door. Then he stopped, for the voice had replied, "Thank you very much," and then a man had walked through the closed, double-locked wooden door.

The man was of medium height, nicely dressed in a gray pin-stripe modified Edwardian suit. His cordovan boots were highly polished. He was black, carried a briefcase, and he had stepped through Edelstein's door as if it had been made of Jell-O.

"Just a minute, stop, hold on one minute," Edelstein said. He found that he was clasping both of his hands together and his heart was beating unpleasantly fast.

The man stood perfectly still and at his ease, one yard within the apartment. Edelstein started to breathe again. He said, "Sorry, I just had a brief attack, a kind of hallucination—"

"Want to see me do it again?" the man asked.

"My God, no! So you *did* walk through the door! Oh, God, I think I'm in trouble."

Edelstein went back to the couch and sat down heavily. The man sat down in a nearby chair.

"What is this all about?" Edelstein whispered.

"I do the door thing to save time," the man said. "It usually closes the credulity gap. My name is Charles Sitwell. I am a field man for the Devil."

Edelstein believed him. He tried to think of a prayer, but all he could remember was the one he used to say over bread in the summer camp he had attended when he was a boy. It probably wouldn't help. He also knew the Lord's Prayer, but that wasn't even his religion. Perhaps the salute to the flag. . . .

"Don't get all worked up," Sitwell said. "I'm not here after your soul or any old-fashioned crap like that."

"How can I believe you?" Edelstein asked.

"Figure it out for yourself," Sitwell told him. "Consider only the war aspect. Nothing but rebellions and revolutions for the past fifty years or so. For us, that means an unprecedented supply of condemned Americans, Viet Cong, Nigerians, Biafrans, Indonesians, South Africans, Russians, Indians, Pakistanis and Arabs. Israelis, too, I'm sorry to tell you. Also, we're pulling in more Chinese than usual, and just recently, we've begun to get plenty of action on the South American market. Speaking frankly, Mr. Edelstein, we're overloaded with souls. If another war starts this year, we'll have to declare an amnesty on venial sins."

Edelstein thought it over. "Then you're really not here to take me to hell?"

"Hell, no!" Sitwell said. "I told you, our waiting list is longer than for Peter Cooper Village; we hardly have any room left in limbo."

"Well. . . . Then why are you here?"

Sitwell crossed his legs and leaned forward earnestly. "Mr. Edelstein, you have to understand that hell is very much like U. S. Steel or I.T.&T. We're a big outfit and we're more or less a monopoly. But, like any really big corporation, we are imbued with the ideal of public service and we like to be well thought of."

"Makes sense," Edelstein said.

"But, unlike Ford, we can't very well establish a foundation and start giving out scholarships and work grants. People wouldn't understand. For the same reason, we can't start building model cities or fighting pollution. We can't even throw up a dam in Afghanistan without someone questioning our motives."

"I see where it could be a problem," Edelstein admitted.

"Yet we like to do something. So, from time to time, but especially now, with business so good, we like to distribute a small bonus to a random selection of potential customers."

"Customer? Me?"

Can You Feel Anything When I Do This? 83

"No one is calling you a sinner," Sitwell pointed out. "I said *potential*— which means everybody."

"Oh. . . . What kind of bonus?"

"Three wishes," Sitwell said briskly. "That's the traditional form."

"Let me see if I've got this straight," Edelstein said. "I can have any three wishes I want? With no penalty, no secret ifs and buts?"

"There is one but," Sitwell said.

"I knew it," Edelstein said.

"It's simple enough. Whatever you wish for, your worst enemy gets double."

Edelstein thought about that. "So if I asked for a million dollars—"

"Your worst enemy would get two million dollars."

"And if I asked for pneumonia?"

"Your worst enemy would get double pneumonia."

Edelstein pursed his lips and shook his head. "Look, not that I mean to tell you people how to run your business, but I hope you realize that you endanger customer good will with a clause like that."

"It's a risk, Mr. Edelstein, but absolutely necessary on a couple of counts," Sitwell said. "You see, the clause is a psychic feedback device that acts to maintain homeostasis."

"Sorry, I'm not following you," Edlestein answered.

"Let me put it this way. The clause acts to reduce the power of the three wishes and, thus, to keep things reasonably normal. A wish is an extremely strong instrument, you know."

"I can imagine," Edelstein said. "Is there a second reason?"

"You should have guessed it already," Sitwell said, baring exceptionally white teeth in an approximation of a smile. "Clauses like that are our trademark. That's how you know it's a genuine hellish product."

"I see, I see," Edelstein said. "Well, I'm going to need some time to think about this."

"The offer is good for thirty days," Sitwell said, standing up. "When you want to make a wish, simply state it—clearly and loudly. I'll tend to the rest."

Sitwell walked to the door. Edelstein said, "There's only one problem I think I should mention."

"What's that?" Sitwell asked.

"Well, it just so happens that I don't have a worst enemy. In fact, I don't have an enemy in the world."

Sitwell laughed hard, then wiped his eyes with a mauve handerkerchief. "Edelstein," he said, "you're really too much! Not an enemy in the world! What about your cousin Seymour, who you wouldn't lend five hundred dollars to, to start a dry-cleaning business? Is he a friend all of a sudden?"

"I hadn't thought about Seymour," Edelstein answered.

"And what about Mrs. Abramowitz, who spits at the mention of your name, because you wouldn't marry her Marjorie? What about Tom Cassiday in apartment 1C of this building, who has a complete collection of Goebbels' speeches and dreams every night of killing all of the Jews in the world, beginning with you? . . . Hey, are you all right?"

Edelstein, sitting on the couch, had gone white and his hands were clasped tightly together again.

"I never realized," he said.

"No one realizes," Sitwell said. "Look, take it easy, six or seven enemies is nothing; I can assure you that you're well below average, hatewise."

"Who else?" Edelstein asked, breathing heavily.

"I'm not going to tell you," Sitwell said. "It would be needless aggravation."

"But I have to know who is my worst enemy! Is it Cassiday? Do you think I should buy a gun?"

Sitwell shook his head. "Cassiday is a harmless, half-witted lunatic. He'll never lift a finger, you have my word on that. Your worst enemy is a man named Edward Samuel Manowitz."

"You're sure of that?" Edelstein asked incredulously.

"Completely sure."

"But Manowitz happens to be my best friend."

"Also your worst enemy," Sitwell replied. "Sometimes

it works like that. Goodbye, Mr. Edelstein, and good luck with your three wishes."

"Wait!" Edelstein cried. He wanted to ask a million questions; but he was embarrassed and he asked only, "How can it be that hell is so crowded?"

"Because only heaven is infinite," Sitwell told him.

"You know about heaven, too?"

"Of course. It's the parent corporation. But now I really must be getting along. I have an appointment in Poughkeepsie. Good luck, Mr. Edelstein."

Sitwell waved and turned and walked out through the locked solid door.

Edelstein sat perfectly still for five minutes. He thought about Eddie Manowitz. His worst enemy! That was laughable; hell had really gotten its wires crossed on that piece of information. He had known Manowitz for twenty years, saw him nearly every day, played chess and gin rummy with him. They went for walks together, saw movies together, at least one night a week they ate dinner together.

It was true, of course, that Manowitz could sometimes open up a big mouth and overstep the boundaries of good taste.

Sometimes Manowitz could be downright rude.

To be perfectly honest, Manowitz had, on more than one occasion, been insulting.

"But we're *friends*," Edelstein said to himself. "We *are* friends, aren't we?"

There was an easy way to test it, he realized. He could wish for $1,000,000. That would give Manowitz $2,000,000. But so what? Would he, a wealthy man, care that his best friend was wealthier?

Yes! He would care! He damned well would care! It would eat his life away if a wise guy like Manowitz got rich on Edelstein's wish.

"My God!" Edelstein thought. "An hour ago, I was a poor but contented man. Now I have three wishes and an enemy."

He found that he was twisting his hands together again. He shook his head. This was going to need some thought.

In the next week, Edelstein managed to get a leave of absence from his job and sat day and night with a pen and pad in his hand. At first, he couldn't get his mind off castles. Castles seemed to go with wishes. But, on second thought, it was not a simple matter. Taking an average dream castle with a ten-foot-thick stone wall, grounds and the rest, one had to consider the matter of upkeep. There was heating to worry about, the cost of several servants, because anything less would look ridiculous.

So it came at last to a matter of money.

I could keep up a pretty decent castle on $2000 a week, Edelstein thought, jotting figures down rapidly on his pad.

But that would mean that Manowitz would be maintaining two castles on $4000 a week!

By the second week, Edelstein had gotten past castles and was speculating feverishly on the endless possibilities and combinations of travel. Would it be too much to ask for a cruise around the world? Perhaps it would; he wasn't even sure he was up to it. Surely he could accept a summer in Europe? Even a two-week vacation at the Fontainebleau in Miami Beach to rest his nerves.

But Manowitz would get two vacations! If Edelstein stayed at the Fontainebleau, Manowitz would have a penthouse suite at the Key Largo Colony Club. Twice.

It was almost better to stay poor and to keep Manowitz deprived.

Almost, but not quite.

During the final week, Edelstein was getting angry and desperate, even cynical. He said to himself, I'm an idiot, how do I know that there's anything to this? So Sitwell could walk through doors; does that make him a magician? Maybe I've been worried about nothing.

He surprised himself by standing up abruptly and saying, in a loud, firm voice, "I want twenty thousand dollars and I want it right now."

Can You Feel Anything When I Do This?

He felt a gentle tug at his right buttock. He pulled out his wallet. Inside it, he found a certified check made out to him for $20,000.

He went down to his bank and cashed the check, trembling, certain that the police would grab him. The manager looked at the check and initialed it. The teller asked him what denominations he wanted it in. Edelstein told the teller to credit it to his account.

As he left the bank, Manowitz came rushing in, an expression of fear, joy and bewilderment on his face.

Edelstein hurried home before Manowitz could speak to him. He had a pain in his stomach for the rest of the day.

Idiot! He had asked for only a lousy $20,000. But Manowitz had gotten $40,000!

A man could die from the aggravation.

Edelstein spent his days alternating between apathy and rage. That pain in the stomach had come back, which meant that he was probably giving himself an ulcer.

It was all so damned unfair! Did he have to push himself into an early grave, worrying about Manowitz?

Yes!

For now he realized that Manowitz was really his enemy and that the thought of enriching his enemy was literally killing him.

He thought about that and then said to himself, Edelstein, listen to me; you can't go on like this, you must get some satisfaction!

But how?

He paced up and down his apartment. The pain was definitely an ulcer; what else could it be?

Then it came to him. Edelstein stopped pacing. His eyes rolled wildly and, seizing paper and pencil, he made some lightning calculations. When he finished, he was flushed, excited—happy for the first time since Sitwell's visit.

He stood up. He shouted, "I want six hundred pounds of chopped chicken liver and I want it at once!"

The caterers began to arrive within five minutes.

Edelstein ate several giant portions of chopped chicken

liver, stored two pounds of it in his refrigerator and sold most of the rest to a caterer at half price, making over $700 on the deal. The janitor had to take away 75 pounds that had been overlooked. Edelstein had a good laugh at the thought of Manowitz standing in his apartment up to his neck in chopped chicken liver.

His enjoyment was short-lived. He learned that Manowitz had kept ten pounds for himself (the man always had had a gross appetite), presented five pounds to a drab little widow he was trying to make an impression on and sold the rest back to the caterer for one third off, earning over $2000.

I am the world's prize imbecile, Edelstein thought. For a minute's stupid satisfaction, I gave up a wish worth conservatively $100,000,000. And what do I get out of it? Two pounds of chopped chicken liver, a few hundred dollars and the lifelong friendship of my janitor!

He knew he was killing himself from sheer brute aggravation.

He was down to one wish now.

And now it was *crucial* that he spend that final wish wisely. But he had to ask for something that he wanted desperately—something that Manowitz would *not* like at all.

Four weeks had gone by. One day, Edelstein realized glumly that his time was just about up. He had racked his brain, only to confirm his worst suspicions: Manowitz liked everything that he liked. Manowitz liked castles, women, wealth, cars, vacations, wine, music, food. Whatever you named, Manowitz the copycat liked it.

Then he remembered: Manowitz, by some strange quirk of the taste buds, could not abide lox.

But Edelstein didn't like lox, either, not even Nova Scotia.

Edelstein prayed: Dear God, who is in charge of hell and heaven, I have had three wishes and used two miserably. Listen, God, I don't mean to be ungrateful, but I ask you, if a man happens to be granted three wishes, shouldn't he be able to do better for himself than I have done? Shouldn't he be able to have something good hap-

Can You Feel Anything When I Do This?

pen to him without filling the pockets of Manowitz, his worst enemy, who does nothing but collect double with no effort or pain?

The final hour arrived. Edelstein grew calm, in the manner of a man who had accepted his fate. He realized that his hatred of Manowitz was futile, unworthy of him. With a new and sweet serenity, he said to himself, I am now going to ask for what I, Edelstein, personally want. If Manowitz has to go along for the ride, it simply can't be helped.

Edelstein stood up very straight. He said, "This is my last wish. I've been a bachelor too long. What I want is a woman whom I can marry. She should be about five feet, four inches tall, weigh about 115 pounds, shapely, of course, and with naturally blonde hair. She should be intelligent, practical, in love with me, Jewish, of course, but sensual and fun-loving—"

The Edelstein mind suddenly moved into high gear!

"And *especially*," he added, "she should be—I don't know quite how to put this—she should be the *most*, the *maximum*, that I want and can handle, speaking now in a purely sexual sense. You understand what I mean, Sitwell? Delicacy forbids that I should spell it out more specifically than that, but if the matter must be explained to you. . . ."

There was a light, somehow *sexual* tapping at the door. Edelstein went to answer it, chuckling to himself. Over twenty thousand dollars, two pounds of chopped chicken liver and now this! Manowitz, he thought, I have you now: Double the most a man wants is something I probably shouldn't have wished on my worst enemy, but I did.

STARTING FROM SCRATCH

Last night I had a very strange dream. I dreamed that a voice said to me, "Excuse me for interrupting your previous dream, but I have an urgent problem and only you can help me with it."

I dreamed that I replied, "No apologies are necessary, it wasn't that good a dream, and if I can help you in any way—"

"*Only* you can help," the voice said. "Otherwise I and all my people are doomed."

"Christ," I said.

His name was Froka and he was a member of a very ancient race. They had lived since time immemorial in a broad valley surrounded by gigantic mountains. They were a peaceable people, and they had, in the course of time, produced some outstanding artists. Their laws were exemplary, and they brought up their children in a loving and permissive manner. Though a few of them tended to indulge in drunkenness, and they had even known an occasional murderer, they considered themselves good and respectable sentient beings, who—

I interrupted. "Look here, can't you get straight to the urgent problem?"

Froka apologized for being long-winded, but explained that on his world the standard form for supplications included a lengthy statement about the moral righteousness of the supplicant.

"Okay," I told him. "Let's get to the problem."

Froka took a deep breath and began. He told me that about one hundred years ago (as they reckon time), an

Can You Feel Anything When I Do This? 91

enormous reddish-yellow shaft had descended from the skies, landing close to the statue to the Unknown God in front of the city hall of their third largest city.

The shaft was imperfectly cylindrical, and about two miles in diameter. It ascended upward beyond the reach of their instruments, and in defiance of all natural laws. They tested and found that the shaft was impervious to cold, heat, bacteria, proton bombardment, and, in fact, everything else they could think of. It stood there, motionless and incredible, for precisely five months, nineteen hours, and six minutes.

Then, for no reason at all, the shaft began to move in a north-northwesterly direction. Its mean speed was 78.881 miles per hour (as they reckon speed). It cut a gash 183.223 miles long by 2.011 miles wide, and then disappeared.

A symposium of scientific authorities could reach no conclusion about this event. They finally declared that it was inexplicable, unique, and unlikely ever to be duplicated.

But it did happen again, a month later, and this time in the capital. This time the cylinder moved a total of 820.331 miles, in seemingly erratic patterns. Property damage was incalculable. Several thousand lives were lost.

Two months and a day after that the shaft returned again, affecting all three major cities.

By this time everyone was aware that not only their individual lives, but their entire civilization, their very existence as a race, was threatened by some unknown and perhaps unknowable phenomenon.

This knowledge resulted in a widespread despair among the general population. There was a rapid alternation between hysteria and apathy.

The fourth assault took place in the wastelands to the east of the capital. Real damage was minimal. Nevertheless, this time there was mass panic, which resulted in a frightening number of deaths by suicide.

The situation was desperate. Now the pseudo-sciences were brought into the struggle alongside the sciences. No help was disdained, no theory was discounted, whether it be by biochemist, palmist, or astronomer. Not even the most outlandish conception could be disregarded, especially after the terrible summer night in which the beautiful ancient city of Raz and its two suburbs were completely annihilated.

"Excuse me," I said, "I'm sorry to hear that you've had all this trouble, but I don't see what it has to do with me."

"I was just coming to that," the voice said.

"Then continue," I said. "But I would advise you to hurry up, because I think I'm going to wake up soon."

"My own part in this is rather difficult to explain," Froka continued. "I am by profession a certified public accountant. But as a hobby I dabble in various techniques for expanding mental perception. Recently I have been experimenting with a chemical compound which we call *kola*, and which frequently causes states of deep illumination—"

"We have similar compounds," I told him.

"Then you understand! Well, while voyaging—do you use that term? While under the influence, so to speak, I obtained a knowledge, a completely far-out understanding . . . But it's so difficult to explain."

"Go on," I broke in impatiently. "Get to the heart of it."

"Well," the voice said, "I realized that my world existed upon many levels—atomic, subatomic, vibrationary planes, an infinity of levels of reality, all of which are also parts of other levels of existence."

"I know about that," I said excitedly. "I recently realized the same thing about my world."

"So it was apparent to me," Froka went on, "that one of our levels was being disturbed."

"Could you be a little more specific?" I said.

"My own feeling is that my world is experiencing an intrusion on a molecular level."

"Wild," I told him. "But have you been able to trace down the intrusion?"

Can You Feel Anything When I Do This? 93

"I think that I have," the voice said. "But I have no proof. All of this is pure intuition."

"I believe in intuition myself," I told him. "Tell me what you've found out."

"Well, sir," the voice said hesitantly, "I have come to realize—intuitively—that my world is a microscopic parasite of you."

"Say it straight!"

"All right! I have discovered that in one aspect, on one plane of reality, my world exists between the second and third knuckles of your left hand. It has existed there for millions of our years, which are minutes to you. I cannot prove this, of course, and I am certainly not accusing you—"

"That's okay," I told him. "You say that your world is located between the second and third knuckles of my left hand. All right. What can I do about it?"

"Well, sir, my guess is that recently you have begun scratching in that area of my world."

"Scratching?"

"I think so."

"And you think that the great destructive reddish shaft is one of my fingers?"

"Precisely."

"And you want me to stop scratching."

"Only near that spot," the voice said hastily. "It is an embarrassing request to make, and I make it only in hopes of saving my world from utter destruction. And I apologize—"

"Don't bother apologizing," I said. "Sentient creatures should be ashamed of nothing."

"It's kind of you to say so," the voice said. "We are nonhuman, you know, and parasites, and we have no claims on you."

"All sentient creatures should stick together," I told him. "You have my word that I will never ever again, so long as I live, scratch between the first and second knuckles of my left hand."

"The second and third knuckles," he reminded me.

"I'll never again scratch between *any* of the knuckles

of my left hand! That is a solemn pledge and a promise which I will keep as long as I have breath."

"Sir," the voice said, "you have saved my world. No thanks could be sufficient. But I thank you nevertheless."

"Don't mention it," I said.

Then the voice went away and I woke up.

As soon as I remembered the dream, I put a Band-Aid across the knuckles of my left hand. I have ignored various itches in that area, have not even washed my left hand. I have worn this Band-Aid for a week.

At the end of next week I am going to take off the Band-Aid. I figure that should give them twenty or thirty billion years as they reckon time, which ought to be long enough for any race.

But that isn't my problem. My problem is that lately I have begun to have some unpleasant intuitions about the earthquakes along the San Andreas Fault, and the renewed volcanic activity in central Mexico. I mean it's all coming together, and I'm scared.

So look, excuse me for interrupting your previous dream, but I have this urgent problem that only you can help me with . . .

THE MNEMONE

It was a great day for our village when the Mnemone arrived. But we did not know him at first, because he concealed his identity from us. He said that his name was Edgar Smith, and that he was a repairer of furniture. We accepted both statements at face value, as we receive all statements. Until then, we had never known anyone who had anything to conceal.

He came into our village on foot, carrying a knapsack and a battered suitcase. He looked at our stores and houses. He walked up to me and asked, "Where is the police station?"

"We have none," I told him.

"Indeed? Then where is the local constable or sheriff?"

"Luke Johnson was constable here for nineteen years," I told him. "But Luke died two years ago. We reported this to the county seat as the law requires. But no one has been sent yet to take his place."

"So you police yourselves?"

"We live quietly," I said. "There's no crime in this village. Why do you ask?"

"Because I wanted to know," Smith said, not very helpfully. "A little knowledge is not as dangerous as a lot of ignorance, eh? Never mind, my blank-faced young friend. I like the look of your village. I like the wooden frame buildings and the stately elms. I like—"

"The stately what?" I asked him.

"Elms," he said, gesturing at the tall trees that lined Main Street. "Didn't you know their name?"

"It was forgotten," I said, embarrassed.

"No matter. Many things have been lost, and some

95

have been hidden. Still, there's no harm in the name of a tree. Or is there?"

"No harm at all," I said. "Elm trees."

"Keep that to yourself," he said, winking. "It's only a morsel, but there's no telling when it might prove useful. I shall stay for a time in this village."

"You are most welcome," I said. "Especially now, at harvest time."

Smith looked at me sharply. "I have nothing to do with that. Did you take me for an itinerant apple-picker?"

"I didn't think about it one way or another. What will you do here?"

"I repair furniture," Smith said.

"Not much call for that in a village this size," I told him.

"Then maybe I'll find something else to turn my hand to." He grinned at me suddenly. "For the moment, however, I require lodgings."

I took him to the Widow Marsini's house, and there he rented her large back bedroom with porch and separate entrance. He arranged to take all of his meals there, too.

His arrival let loose a flood of gossip and speculation. Mrs. Marsini felt that Smith's questions about the police went to show that he himself was a policeman. "They work like that," she said. "Or they used to. Back fifty years ago, every third person you met was some kind of a policeman. Sometimes even your own children were policemen, and they'd be as quick to arrest you as they would a stranger. Quicker!"

But others pointed out that all of that had happened long ago, that life was quiet now, that policemen were rarely seen, even though they were still believed to exist.

But why had Smith come? Some felt that he was here to take something from us. "What other reason is there for a stranger to come to a village like this?" And others felt that he had come to give us something, citing the same argument.

But we didn't know. We simply had to wait until Smith chose to reveal himself.

He moved among us as other men do. He had knowledge of the outside world; he seemed to us a far-traveling man. And slowly, he began to give us clues as to his identity.

One day I took him to a rise which looks out over our valley. This was at midautumn, a pretty time. Smith looked out and declared it a fine sight. "It puts me in mind of that famous tag from William James," he said. "How does it go? 'Scenery seems to wear in one's consciousness better than any other element in life.' Eh? Apt, don't you think?"

"Who is or was this William James?" I asked.

Smith winked at me. "Did I mention that name? Slip of the tongue, my lad."

But that was not the last "slip of the tongue." A few days later I pointed out an ugly hillside covered with second-growth pine, low coarse shrubbery, and weeds. "This burned five years ago," I told him. "Now it serves no purpose at all."

"Yes, I see," Smith said. "And yet—as Montaigne tells us—there is nothing useless in nature, not even uselessness itself."

And still later, walking through the village, he paused to admire Mrs. Vogel's late-blooming peonies. He said, "Flowers do indeed have the glances of children and the mouths of old men . . . Just as Chazal pointed out."

Toward the end of the week, a few of us got together in the back of Edmonds's Store and began to discuss Mr. Edgar Smith. I mentioned the things he had said to me. Bill Edmonds remembered that Smith had cited a man named Emerson, to the effect that solitude was impracticable, and society fatal. Billy Foreclough told us that Smith had quoted Ion of Chios to him: that Luck differs greatly from Art, yet creates many things that are like it. And Mrs. Gordon suddenly came up with the best of the lot; a statement Smith told her was made by the great Leonardo da Vinci: vows begin when hope dies.

We looked at each other and were silent. It was evident to everyone that Mr. Edgar Smith—or whatever his real name might be—was no simple repairer of furniture.

At last I put into words what we were all thinking. "Friends," I said, "this man appears to be a Mnemone."

Mnemones as a distinct class came into prominence during the last year of the War Which Ended All Wars. Their self-proclaimed function was to remember works of literature which were in danger of being lost, destroyed, or suppressed.

At first, the government welcomed their efforts, encouraged them, even rewarded them with pensions and grants. But when the war ended and the reign of the Police Presidents began, government policy changed. A general decision was made to jettison the unhappy past, to build a new world in and of the present. Disturbing influences were to be struck down without mercy.

Right-thinking men agreed that most literature was superfluous at best, subversive at worst. After all, was it necessary to perserve the mouthings of a thief like Villon, a homosexual like Genet, a schizophrenic like Kafka? Did we need to retain a thousand divergent opinions, and then to explain why they were false? Under such a bombardment of influences, how could anyone be expected to respond in an appropriate and approved manner? How would one ever get people to obey orders?

The government knew that if everyone obeyed orders, everything would be all right.

But to achieve this blessed state, divergent and ambiguous inputs had to be abolished. The biggest single source of confusing inputs came from historical and artistic verbiage. Therefore, history was to be rewritten, and literature was to be regularized, pruned, tamed, made orderly or abolished entirely.

Can You Feel Anything When I Do This? 99

The Mnemones were ordered to leave the past strictly alone. They objected to this most vehemently, of course. Discussions continued until the government lost patience. A final order was issued, with heavy penalties for those who would not comply.

Most of the Mnemones gave up their work. A few only pretended to, however. These few became an elusive, persecuted minority of itinerant teachers, endlessly on the move, selling their knowledge where and when they could.

We questioned the man who called himself Edgar Smith, and he revealed himself to us as a Mnemone. He gave immediate and lavish gifts to our village:

Two sonnets by William Shakespeare.

Job's Lament to God.

One entire act of a play by Aristophanes.

This done, he set himself up in business, offering his wares for sale to the villagers.

He drove a hard bargain with Mr. Ogden, forcing him to exchange an entire pig for two lines of Simonides.

Mr. Bellington, the recluse, gave up his gold watch for a saying by Heraclitus. He considered it a fair exchange.

Old Mrs. Heath exchanged a pound of goosefeathers for three stanzas from a poem entitled "Atalanta in Calydon," by a man named Swinburne.

Mr. Mervin, who owns the restaurant, purchased an entire short ode by Catullus, a description of Cicero by Tacitus, and ten lines from Homer's Catalogue of Ships. This cost his entire savings.

I had little in the way of money or property. But for services rendered, I received a paragraph of Montaigne, a saying ascribed to Socrates, and ten fragmentary lines by Anacreon.

An unexpected customer was Mr. Lind, who came stomping into the Mnemone's office one crisp winter morning. Mr. Lind was short, red-faced, and easily moved to anger. He was the most successful farmer in the area, a man of no nonsense who believed only in what he could see and touch. He was the last man whom you'd ever expect to buy the Mnemone's wares. Even a policeman would have been a more likely prospect.

"Well, well," Lind began, rubbing his hands briskly together. "I've heard about you and your invisible merchandise."

"And I've heard about you," the Mnemone said, with a touch of malice to his voice. "Do you have business with me?"

"Yes, by God, I do!" Lind cried. "I want to buy some of your fancy old words."

"I am genuinely surprised," the Mnemone said. "Who would ever have dreamed of finding a law-abiding citizen like yourself in a situation like this, buying goods which are not only invisible, but illegal as well!"

"It's not my choice," Lind said. "I have come here only to please my wife, who is not well these days."

"Not well? I'm not surprised," the Mnemone said. "An ox would sicken under the workload you give her."

"Man, that's no concern of yours!" Lind said furiously.

"But it is," the Mnemone said. "In my profession we do not give out words at random. We fit our lines to the recipient. Sometimes we find nothing appropriate, and therefore sell nothing at all."

"I thought you sold your wares to all buyers."

"You have been misinformed. I know a Pindaric ode I would not sell to you for any price."

"Man, you can't talk to me that way!"

"I speak as I please. You are free to take your business somewhere else."

Mr. Lind glowered and pouted and sulked, but there was nothing he could do. At last he said, "I didn't mean to lose my temper. Will you sell me something for my wife? Last week was her birthday, but I didn't remember it until just now."

"You are a pretty fellow," the Mnemone said. "As sentimental as a mink, and almost as loving as a shark!

Why come to me for her present? Wouldn't a sturdy butter churn be more suitable?"

"No, not so," Lind said, his voice flat and quiet. "She lies in bed this past month and barely eats. I think she is dying."

"And she asked for words of mine?"

"She asked me to bring her something pretty."

The Mnemone nodded. "Dying! Well, I'll offer no condolences to the man who drove her to the grave, and I've not much sympathy for the woman who picked a creature like you. But I do have something she will like, a gaudy thing that will ease her passing. It'll cost you a mere thousand dollars."

"God in heaven, man! Have you nothing cheaper?"

"Of course I have," the Mnemone said. "I have a decent little comic poem in Scots dialect with the middle gone from it; yours for two hundred dollars. And I have one stanza of a commemorative ode to General Kitchener which you can have for ten dollars."

"Is there nothing else?"

"Not for you."

"Well . . . I'll take the thousand dollar item," Lind said. "Yes, by God, I will! Sara is worth every penny of it!"

"Handsomely said, albeit tardily. Now pay attention. Here it is."

The Mnemone leaned back, closed his eyes, and began to recite. Lind listened, his face tense with concentration. And I also listened, cursing my untrained memory and praying that I would not be ordered from the room.

It was a long poem, and very strange and beautiful. I still possess it all. But what comes most often to my mind are the lines

Charm'd magic casements, opening on the foam
Of perilous seas, in faery lands forlorn.

We are men: queer beasts with strange appetites. Who would have imagined us to possess a thirst for the ineffable? What was the hunger that could lead a man to exchange three bushels of corn for a single saying of the Gnostics? To feast on the spiritual—this seems to be what men must do; but who could have imagined it of *us*? Who would have thought us sufferers of malnutrition because we had no Plato? Can a man grow sickly from lack of Plutarch, or die from an Aristotle deficiency?

I cannot deny it. I myself have seen the results of abruptly withdrawing an addict from Strindberg.

Our past is a necessary part of us, and to take away that part is to mutilate us irreparably. I know a man who achieved courage only after he was told of Epaminondas, and a woman who became beautiful only after she heard of Aphrodite.

The Mnemone had a natural enemy in our schoolteacher, Mr. Vich, who taught the authorized version of all things. The Mnemone also had an enemy in Father Dulces, who ministered to our spiritual needs in the Universal Patriotic Church of America.

The Mnemone defied both of our authorities. He told us that many of the things they taught us were false, both in content and in ascription, or were perversions of famous sayings, rephrased to say the opposite of the original author's intention. The Mnemone struck at the very foundations of our civilization when he denied the validity of the following sayings:

—Most men lead lives of quite aspiration.
—The unexamined life is most worth living.
—Know thyself within approved limits.

We listened to the Mnemone, we considered what he told us. Slowly, painfully, we began to think again, to reason, to examine things for ourselves. And when we did this, we also began to hope.

The neoclassical flowering of our village was brief, intense, sudden, and a delight to us all. Only one thing warned me that the end might be imminent. There was a day in early spring when I had been helping one of

Can You Feel Anything When I Do This?   103

the neighbor's children with his lessons. He had a new edition of Dunster's *General History,* and I glanced through the section on the Silver Age of Rome. It took me a few minutes to realize that Cicero had been omitted. He wasn't even listed in the index, though many lesser poets and orators were. I wondered what retrospective crime he had been found guilty of.

And then one day, quite suddenly, the end came. Three men entered our village. They wore gray uniforms with brass insignia. Their faces were blank and broad, and they walked stiffly in heavy black boots. They went everywhere together, and they always stood very close to one another. They asked no questions. They spoke to no one. They knew exactly where the Mnemone lived, and they consulted a map and then walked directly there.

They were in Smith's room for perhaps ten minutes.

Then the three policemen came out again into the street, all three of them walking together like one man. Their eyes darted right and left; they seemed frightened. They left our village quickly.

We buried Smith on a rise of land overlooking the valley, near the place where he had first quoted William James, among late-blooming flowers which had the glances of children and the mouths of old men.

Mrs. Blake, in a most untypical gesture, has named her latest-born Cicero. Mr. Lind refers to his apple orchard as Xanadu. I myself have become an avowed Zoroastrian, entirely on faith, since I know nothing about that religion except that it directs a man to speak the truth and shoot the arrow straight.

But these are futile gestures. The truth is, we have lost Xanadu irretrievably, lost Cicero, lost Zoroaster. And what else have we lost? What great battles were fought, cities built, jungles conquered? What songs were sung, what dreams were dreamed? We see it now, too late, that our intelligence is a plant which must be rooted in the rich fields of the past.

In brief, our collective memories, the richest part of us, have been taken away, and we are poor indeed. In return for castles of the mind, our rulers have given us mud hovels palpable to the touch; a bad exchange for us.

The Mnemone, by official proclamation, never existed. By fiat he is ranked as an inexplicable dream or delusion—like Cicero. And I who write these lines, I too will soon cease to exist. Like Cicero and the Mnemone, my reality will also be proscribed.

Nothing will help me: the truth is too fragile, it shatters too easily in the iron hands of our rulers. I shall not be revenged. I shall not even be remembered. For if the great Zoroaster himself could be reduced to a single rememberer, and that one killed, then what hope is there for me?

Generation of cows! Sheep! Pigs! We have not even the spirit of a goat! If Epaminondas was a man, if Achilles was a man, if Socrates was a man, then are we also men?

TRIPOUT

1

Papazian appeared, disguised as a human being. He checked quickly to make sure that his head was on right. "Nose and toes the same way goes," he reminded himself, and that was how it was.

All of his systems were go. His psyche was soldered firmly to his pineal gland, and he even had a small soul powered by flashlight batteries. He was on Earth, a weird place, in New York, crossroads of ten million private lives. He tried to gropple, but this body wouldn't do it. So he smiled, an adequate substitute.

He left the telephone booth and went out into the street to play with the people.

2

The first person he met was a fat man of about forty. The man stopped him and said, "Hey, bud, what's the quickest way to 49th Street and Broadway?"

Papazian answered without hesitation, "Feel along that wall until you hit a soft spot. Then step through. It's a spatial bypass which the Martians put in, back when there were Martians— It'll take you out at 48th Street and Seventh Avenue, which I call pretty good service."

"Snotty wise guy bastard," the man said, and walked away without even touching the wall to see if there was a soft spot.

Much characterological rigidity, Papazian said to himself. *I must include that in my report.*

But was he supposed to make a report? He didn't

know. But, of course, he didn't worry about it. Such things tended to manifest themselves.

3

Lunchtime! Papazian went to a run-down sleazy diner on Broadway near 28th Street. He said to the counterman, "I'll have one of your famous hot dogs, please."

"Famous?" the counterman sneered. "That'll be the day."

"Then this is the day," Papazian replied. "Your hot dogs have a galaxy-wide reputation. I know beings who have traveled a thousand light-years solely to eat those hot dogs."

"Nut," the counterman said.

"Nut, am I? It may interest you to know that half of your customers at this moment are extraterrestrial beings. In disguise, of course."

Half the customers at the lunch counter turned pale.

"What are you, some kind of foreigner?" the counterman asked.

"I'm Aldebaranese on my mother's side," Papazian said.

"That accounts for it," the counterman said.

4

Papazian walked down the street knowing nothing. He was really enjoying his ignorance. His own ignorance excited him. It meant that he had a lot of things to learn. It was so marvelous, not to know what you were going to do next, or be, or say.

"Hey, bud," a man called out, "will this subway take me to Washington Heights?"

"I don't know," Papazian said, and it was true, he didn't know, he didn't even know how to get to Washington Heights! It was a pinnacle in the annals of ignorance.

But no one can stay *that* ignorant for long. A woman hurried over and told them how to get to Washington Heights. Papazian found it mildly interesting, but not as interesting as not knowing.

5

The sign on the building said LOFT FOR RENT.

Papazian went in at once and rented it. He thought that was the proper move. But he hoped it was the improper move, which was bound to be more amusing.

6

The young woman said, "Good day, I am Miss Marsh. The agency sent me. They said you needed a secretary."

"That is correct. You are hired."

"Just like that?"

"I can't think of any other way. What is your first name?"

"Lillian."

"That is satisfactory. Please begin working."

"But you don't have any furniture here, not even a typewriter."

"Get what you require. Here is money."

"But what am I supposed to *do?*"

"You mustn't ask me that," Papazian said gently. "I find it hard enough to find out what I am supposed to do. Surely you can run your own life?"

"What are you supposed to do, Mr. Papazian?"

"I am supposed to discover what I am supposed to do."

"Oh . . . Well, all right. I guess you'll need desks, chairs, lamps, a typewriter, other stuff."

"Marvelous, Lil! I had the feeling that you knew what you were supposed to do all along. Were you aware that you are a very pretty young lady?"

"No . . ."

"Then perhaps you aren't. If you don't know, how can I tell?"

7

Papazian woke up and changed his name to Hal. He was in the Village Central Hotel. He had spent an exciting evening listening to the cockroaches rap about the tenants. Cockroaches are natural mimics and can be extremely funny.

Hal sloughed a layer of skin and left it under the bed for the chambermaid. It was faster than washing.

He went to his loft. Lillian was already there, and some furniture had arrived. Lillian said, "There's a customer in the anteroom, Mr. Papazian."

"I've changed my name to Hal," Hal said. "Send in the customer."

The customer was a short round man named Jaspers.

"What can I do for you, Mr. Jaspers?" Hal asked.

"I haven't the slightest idea," Jaspers said. "Some unaccountable impulse sent me here."

Hal remembered now that he had forgotten where he had left his Unaccountable Impulse Machine.

"Where did you get this unaccountable impulse?" Hal asked.

"On the northeast corner of Fifth Avenue and 18th Street."

"Near the mailbox? I thought so! You have done me a service, Mr. Jaspers! How may I help you?"

"I told you, I don't know. It was an unaccountable—"

"Yes. But what would you like?"

"Time," Jaspers said sadly. "Isn't that what we all would like?"

"No, it is not," Hal said firmly. "But still, maybe I can help you. How much time do you want?"

"I'd like another hundred years," Jaspers said.

"Come back tomorrow," Hal said. "I'll see what I can do for you."

After Jaspers had gone, Lillian asked, "Can you really do something for him?"

"Find out tomorrow," Hal said.

"Why tomorrow?"

"Why not tomorrow?"

"Because you've left Mr. Jaspers and me hanging, and that's not nice."

"No, it is not," Hal admitted. "But it *is* extremely lifelike. I have observed in my travels that life is precisely the state of hanging. The moral is, you must enjoy everything while hanging, because hanging is all you'll ever be able to do."

"Oh, dear, that's too deep for me."

"Then go type a letter, or whatever it is you think you're supposed to do."

8

Hal went down to the Orange Julius on 8th street for lunch. That particular stand had been recommended in the Interplanetary Gourmet's Guide to Inexpensive Eating on Earth. Hal found the chili dog superb. He finished and walked to the southeast corner of Sixth Avenue and 8th Street.

A man with an American flag was standing outside of Nathan's. A small crowd had gathered. The man was old, and he had a red, seamed face. He was saying, "I tell you that the dead live, and that they are walking the earth this very minute. What do you say to that, eh?"

"Personally," Hal replied, "I would have to agree with you, because there is an old gray-haired woman with a withered arm standing beside you in her astral body."

"My God, it must be Ethel! She died last year, mister, and I've been trying to speak to her ever since! What is she saying?"

"She said, and I quote, 'Herbert, stop talking a lot of shit and get back to the apartment on account of that pot of water you left on the stove to boil eggs in hasn't no water left in it and the whole damned place is going to burn down in another half hour.'"

"That's Ethel, all right!" Herbert said. "Ethel! How can you still claim that I am talking shit when you are now a ghost yourself?"

"She said," Hal said, "that a man who can't even boil eggs without burning down his apartment isn't likely to know much about spirits."

"She always got me with her lousy non sequiturs," Herbert said. "Thanks for the help, mister."

He hurried off. Hal said, "Ma'am, weren't you a little hard on him?"

Ethel replied, "He never listened to me when I was alive and he won't now that I'm dead. What could be too hard on a man like that? Nice talking to you, mister, I gotta go now."

"Where?" Hal asked.

"Back to the Home for Aged Spirits, where else?" She departed invisibly.

Hal shook his head in admiration. *Earth!* he thought. *It's an exciting place. Too bad it has to be destroyed.*

He walked on. Then he thought, *Does it have to be destroyed?*

He realized that he didn't know. And that also made him happy.

9

Hal took the spatial bypass from West 16th Street to Cathedral Parkway. He had to change once at Yucca, Arizona, a town well-known for possessing the world's oldest free-standing silo.

Cathedral Parkway had ten colossal cathedrals—gifts to the people of Earth from the religious reptiles of Sainne II. The cathedrals were disguised as brownstones in order to avoid trouble with the local authorities.

Many people were sightseeing today. There were Venusians disguised as Germans, and Sagittarians disguised as hippies. No one likes to be taken for a tourist.

Disquieting note: A fat man (unrelated to any of the other fat men previously encountered) came up to Hal and said, "Excuse me, aren't you Hal Papazian?"

Hal looked the man over. He could perceive a slight discoloration on the man's liver, nothing serious, call it a liver spot. Aside from that, the man seemed to be without distinguishing characteristics, except for fatness.

"I'm Arthur Ventura," the man said. "I am your next-door neighbor.

"You're from Aldebaran?" Hal inquired.

"No, I'm from the Bronx, just like you."

"There is no Bronx on Aldebaran," Hal stated, although he wasn't much in the mood for simple declarative sentences.

"Hal, snap out of it. You've been gone nearly a week.

Ellen is nearly out of her head with worry. She's going to call the police."

"Ellen?"

"Your wife."

Hal knew what was happening. He was having a genuine Confrontation Scene, and also an Identity Crisis. Those were things that the average extraterrestrial tourist never experienced. What a treasured memory this would be, if only he could remember the memory!

"Well," Hal said, "I thank you most kindly for this piece of information. I am sorry to have troubled my wife, sweet Melon—"

"Ellen," Ventura corrected.

"Hmmm, yes. Tell her I will be seeing her as soon as I have completed my task."

"What task is that?"

"Discovery of my task is my task. It is like that with us higher life forms."

Hal smiled and tried to walk away. But Arthur Ventura showed a peculiar *swarming* ability and surrounded Papazian on all sides, and made noises and rushed in reinforcements. Papazian considered inventing a laser beam and killing them all, but of course that would not have been in the spirit of the occasion.

So, by easy stages, aided by various persons, some wearing uniforms, Papazian was brought to an apartment in the Bronx, and a woman fell into his arms weeping and saying various things of a personal and tendentious nature.

Hal deduced that this woman was Ellen. This was the woman who claimed to be his wife. And she had papers to prove it.

10

At first it was fun to have a wife and an assortment of children and a real honest-to-goodness job, and a bank account, and a car, and several changes of clothing, and all the other things that Earthmen have. Hal played with all of the new things. He was able to perform the role of

Ellen's husband without much difficulty: all of the clues were there for him to pick up on.

Almost every day she would ask him, "Honey, can't you really remember anything?"

And Hal would say, "It's all gone. But I'm sure I'll get it back."

Ellen would cry. Hal went along with that, too. He was in no position to make value judgments.

The neighbors were most solicitous, friends were most kind. Everyone made great efforts to conceal their knowledge that he was out of his mind, insane, crazy, a lunatic.

Hal Papazian learned all of the things that Hal Papazian had once done, and did them. He found even the simplest things thrilling. For what greater experience could there be for an Aldebaranese tourist than to live the life of a Terran, and to be accepted as a Terran by other Terrans?

He made mistakes, of course. Doing things at the proper times was difficult for him. But he gradually learned that he should not mow the lawn at midnight, should not wake the children up for their nap at 5 A.M., should not leave for work at 9 P.M. He could see no reason for these restrictions, but they did make matters more interesting.

11

At Ellen's request, Papazian went to see a certain Dr. Kardoman, a person who specialized in reading people's minds and telling them which of their thoughts were true and good and fruitful and which were false and evil and counterproductive.

KARDOMAN: How long have you had the feeling that you are an extraterrestrial person?

PAPAZIAN: It started shortly after my birth on Aldebaran.

KARDOMAN: You would save us both a lot of time if you would simply realize and face the fact that you are a crazy person with a lot of weirdo ideas.

PAPAZIAN: It might also save time if *you* admitted that I am in fact an Aldebaranese male in an unusual situation.

KARDOMAN: Fuck that noise. Listen to me, buster, this pretense will get you nowhere. Stick to my premises and I'll normalize you.

PAPAZIAN: Fuck that noise.

12

The healing process went on apace. Night came, succeeded by day. Week came, subsumed under month. Hal had moments of insight, which Dr. Kardoman applauded, and which Ellen recorded in her manuscript entitled: *Return from Deepest Space; One Woman's Account of Her Life With a Man Who Believed He was from Aldebaran.*

13

One day Hal said to Dr. Kardoman, "Hey, I think my past is coming back to me?"

"Hmmm," said Dr. Kardoman.

"I have a bittersweet memory of myself at the age of eight, serving cocoa to an iron flamingo on my parents' lawn, near the little secret bower where Mavis Healey and I conducted delicious and shameful experiments, and where, not a hundred yards away, the Chesapeake River flowed inexorably into the flaccid depths of Chesapeake Bay."

"Screen memory," Kardoman commented, consulting the dossier which Ellen had put together for him. "At the age of eight you were living in Youngstown, Ohio."

"Damn," Papazian said.

"But you are going the right way," Kardoman told him. "Everybody has screen memories, which conceal the horror and pleasure of whatever true experience must be shielded from the shrinking psyche."

"I knew it was too good to be true," Papazian said.

"Do not discount it. Your screen memory was a helpful indication."

"Good of you to say so," Hal said. "But now, back to the old psychic drawing board."

14

He came up with various other recollections: of his

young manhood spent as a cabin boy aboard a British gunboat on the Yangtze Patrol; of his sixth birthday, celebrated at the Winter Palace in St. Petersburg; of his twenty-fifth year, when he worked as a short-order cook in the Klondike.

These were all indisputably Terran memories; but they were not the memories that Dr. Kardoman was looking for.

15

And then, one fine day, a brush salesman came to the door and asked to speak to the "lady of the house."

"She won't be back for a few hours," Papazian said. "Today is her lesson in demotic Greek, and after that she has a class in intaglio."

"Fine," said the salesman. "I actually wanted to speak to you."

"I don't want any brushes," Papazian said.

"To hell with brushes," the brush salesman said. "I am your holiday liaison officer and I am here to advise you that we are lifting off in exactly four hours."

"Lifting off?"

"All good things must come to an end, even this holiday."

"Holiday?"

"Snap out of it," the brush salesman, or holiday liaison officer said. "You Aldebaranese are really too much."

"Where are you from?"

"Arcturus. We run a tauter psyche on Arcturus, and we never let our memories slide."

"We Aldebaranese always let our memories slide," Papazian said.

"That's why I am a holiday liaison officer and you are a tourist. Have you had a nice time playing with the natives?"

"I seem to have married one," Papazian said. "Or to be more precise, I seem to be the mate of one who once had a mate who looked exactly like me."

"We provided that," the Arcturan said. "A genuine Terran mate, it was part of the tour package. Now, are you coming?"

Can You Feel Anything When I Do This? 115

"It will hurt poor Melon's feelings," Papazian said.

"Her name is Ellen, and she, like most Terrans, spends an incredible amount of time having hurt feelings. I cannot force you to return. If you wish to stay on, another cruise ship will be along in fifty or sixty years."

"To hell with that," Papazian said. "I'll race you back to the ship."

16

The spaceship had been cleverly disguised to look exactly like Fairlawn, New Jersey. The real Fairlawn, New Jersey, had been clearly lifted out and put down in India's Rajasthan province. No one had noticed the difference except the Israelis, who had promptly sent a rabbi and a guerrilla-warfare expert.

"But I still can't remember anything," Hal complained to the holiday liaison officer.

"That's natural. You left your memory bank in a locker aboard the ship."

"What did I do that for?"

"In order not to feel out of place. Your old memories fit right over your present memories. I'll help you sort them out."

Everybody was aboard and alive and well except for the inevitable few who had been killed in South American seaports. These unfortunates would be reconstituted later. Except for the hangover, they would be none the worse for the experience.

The ship lifted off promptly at midnight. The flight was noted by the U. S. Air Force Detection Corps at Scrapple, Pennsylvania. They explained the radar images as being a large accumulation of marsh gas, complicated by a dense flight of swallows.

Despite the nasty chill of outer space, Hal stayed at the rail and watched Earth recede into the distance. He was going back to the humdrum life of a partial-systems photognomic configurator, back to the wives and kiddy, back to the importunities of rust and lichen.

But he left without real regret. He knew that Earth was a nice enough place for a vacation; but one couldn't really live there.

NOTES ON THE PERCEPTION OF IMAGINARY DIFFERENCES

1

Hans and Pierre are in prison. Pierre is a Frenchman, Hans is a German. Pierre is short and plump with black hair. Hans is tall and thin with blond hair. Pierre has sallow skin and a black mustache. Hans is twelve inches shorter than Hans, who is a foot taller than Pierre.

2

Hans and Pierre have just heard that a general amnesty has been declared. Under the terms of the amnesty, Pierre will be released immediately. No mention was made of Germans, so Hans will have to stay in prison. This saddens both men. And they think, if only we could get Hans out instead of Pierre . . .

(Hans, the German prisoner, is an expert locksmith. Once outside, he could rescue his friend from the prison. The Frenchman is a professor of astrophysics and is unable to help anyone, even himself. He is a useless man, but a pleasant one; the German considers him the finest human being he has ever met. Hans is determined to be released from prison in order to help his friend to escape.)

There is a way to accomplish this. If they can deceive the guard into believing that Hans is Pierre, then Hans will be released. Hans will then be able to return to the prison and help Pierre to escape. To this end they have formulated a plan.

Can You Feel Anything When I Do This? 117

Now they hear the sound of footsteps coming down the corridor. It is the guard! They put the first phase of their plan into action by exchanging mustaches.

3

The guard enters the cell and says, "Hans, step forth."
Both men step forth.
The guard says, "Which is Hans?"
Both prisoners answer, "Me."

The guard looks them over. He sees a tall, thin blond man with a black mustache and a fair complexion, standing beside a short, plump, black-haired man with a blond mustache and a sallow complexion. He stares at them suspiciously for several seconds, then picks out the tall man as the German and orders the other man, the Frenchman, to come along.

The prisoners have been prepared for this. Quickly they dart behind the guard and exchange toupees.

The guard looks them over, grins, unalarmed, and checks his prisoner identification list. He decides that the tall, black-haired, black-mustached man with the clear-skinned leanness is the German.

The prisoners confer in whispers. They run around behind the guard. Hans kneels and Pierre stands on his toes. The guard, who is very stupid, slowly turns around to look at them.

It is not so easy this time. He sees two men of identical height. One has blond hair, blond mustache, sallow skin, plumpness. The other has black hair, black mustache, fair skin, thinness. Both men have blue eyes, a coincidence.

After some reflection, the guard decides that the first man, the blond-haired, blond-mustached, sallow-skinned, plump one, is the Frenchman.

The two prisoners slip away again behind his back and dropsy, fallen arches; his reactions have been impaired due to scarlet fever suffered in his youth. He turns slowly, hold a hasty conference. (The guard has bad eyesight, blinking.)

The prisoners exchange mustaches again. The sallow

man pats dust onto his skin, while the light man darkens his face with soot. The plump one stands up higher on his toes, and the thin one slouches down lower on his knees.

The guard sees one plump man of slightly above average height, with a black mustache, blond hair, and light skin. To his left is a sallow fellow of slightly below average height, with a blond mustache and black hair. The guard stares at them hard, frowns, purses his lips, takes out his instructions and reads them again. Then he picks out the light-skinned man of slightly above average height with the black mustache as the Frenchman.

The prisoners scurry away, and the taller man ties his belt tightly around his waist, while the shorter man loosens his belt and stuffs rags under it. They decide to exchange hair and mustaches again, just for luck.

The guard notices at once that the plumpness-thinness factor has diminished in importance. He decides to match up blond-dark characteristics, but then observes that the blond-haired man has a black mustache, while the dark-haired man has a blond mustache. The blond man is slightly below average height, and his skin could be considered sallow. The man on his right has dark hair and blond mustache (slightly askew) and a clearish skin, and he is slightly above average height.

The guard can find nothing in the rules to cover this. Frantic, he takes an old edition of *Prisoner Identification Procedures* from his pocket, searches for something relevant. Finally he finds the notorious Regulation 12CC of 1878: "The French prisoner shall always stand to the left, the German prisoner to the right."

"You," the guard says, pointing to the prisoner on the left. "Come with me, Frenchie. As for you, Kraut, you stay here in the cell."

4

The guard marches his prisoner outside, fills in various papers, and releases him.

Later that night, the remaining prisoner escapes.

(It is easy: the guard is disastrously stupid, not only stupid, he drinks himself into a drunken stupor every night, and takes sleeping pills besides. He is an incredible guard, but it is all easily explainable—he is the son of a famous attorney and Party member. As a favor to his father the authorities gave this job to his incompetent and physically handicapped son. They also decided that he could do it alone. That is why there is no other guard to relieve him, no commandant to check up on him. No, he is all alone, drunk, filled with sleeping pills, and nobody on Earth can awaken him while the prison break is taking place, and that is my last word on the subject of the guard.)

5

The two former prisoners are sitting on a park bench some miles from the prison. They still look as they looked when we saw them last.

One says, "I told you it would work! With you on the outside—"

"Of course it worked," said the other. "I knew it was for the best when the guard picked me, since you could escape from your cell anyhow."

"Now just a minute," said the first man. "Are you trying to say that the guard, despite our deceptions, took away a Frenchman instead of a German?"

"That's it," the second man said. "And it didn't matter which of us the guard took, because if the locksmith was released, he could come back and help the professor; whereas if the professor is released, the locksmith can get out by himself. You see, there was no need for us to swap roles, so we didn't."

The first man glared at him. "I think that you are trying to steal my French identity!"

"Why would I do that?" the second man asked.

"Because you wish to be French, like me. That is only natural, since there in the distance is Paris, where it is an advantage to be a Frenchman, but no help at all to be a German."

"Of course I wish to be a Frenchman," said the second man. "But that is because I am a Frenchman. And that city out there is Limoges, not Paris."

The first man is slightly above average height, dark haired, blond mustache, fair skin, on the thin side. The second man is below average height, has blond hair, black mustache, sallow complexion, and is on the plump side.

They look each other in the eye. They can find no distortion or blemish there. Each man looks at the other straightforwardly, and perceives the honesty in the other's eyes. If neither man is lying, then one of them must be suffering from a delusion.

"If neither of us is lying," said the first man, "then one of us must be suffering from a delusion."

"Agreed," said the second man. "And, since we are both honest men, all we have to do is retrace the steps of the disguise. If we do that, we will arrive back at the original state in which one of us was the short, blond German and the other was the tall, dark Frenchman."

"Yes . . . But was it not the Frenchman who had the blond hair and the German who was tall?"

"That is not my recollection of it," said the second man. "But I think that the harshness of prison life may have affected my memory, to the point where I cannot be sure that I remember which are the German qualities and which are the French. Still, I am perfectly willing to discuss the various points with you and to agree to whatever seems reasonable."

"Well, then, let's simply make up our minds, then we can sort out this ridiculous mess. Shouldn't a German have blond hair?"

"That's all right with me. Give him a blond mustache, too, it matches."

"What about skin?"

"Sallow, definitely. Germany has a damp climate."

"Color of eyes?"

"Blue."

"Plump or thin?"

"Plump, decidedly plump."

"That makes the German tall, blond, sallow and plump, with blue eyes."

"A detail or two may be wrong, but let it stand. Now

Can You Feel Anything When I Do This?

let us trace back and figure out which of us originally looked that way."

6

At first glance, the two men may seem identical, or at least interchangeable. This is a false impression; it must always be remembered that the differences between them are real, no matter which man has which qualities. The differences are perfectly real despite being imaginary. These are imaginary qualities which anyone can perceive, and which make one man a German and the other man a Frenchman.

7

The way to perceive imaginary differences is this: you fix in mind the original qualities of each man, and then you list each of the interchanges. Finally you will arrive at the beginning, and you will know infallibly which is the imaginary German and which is the imaginary Frenchman.

Basically, it is as simple as that. What you do with this knowledge is a different matter, of course.

DOWN THE DIGESTIVE TRACT AND INTO THE COSMOS WITH MANTRA, TANTRA, AND SPECKLEBANG

"But will I really have hallucinations?" Gregory asked.

"Like I said, I guarantee it," Blake answered. "You should be into something by now."

Gregory looked around. The room was dismayingly, tediously familiar: narrow blue bed, walnut dresser, marble table with wrought-iron base, double-headed lamp, turkey-red rug, beige television set. He was sitting in an upholstered armchair. Across from him, on a white plastic couch, was Blake, pale and plump, poking at three speckled irregularly shaped tablets.

"I mean to say," Blake said, "that there's all sorts of acid going around—tabs, strips, blotters, dots, most of it cut with speed and some of it cut with Drano. But lucky you have just ingested old Doc Blake's special tantric mantric instant freakout special superacid cocktail, known to the carriage trade as Specklebang, and containing absolutely simon-pure LSD-25, plus carefully calculated additives of STP, DMT, and THC, plus a smidgen of Yage, a touch of psilocybin, and the merest hint of oloiuqui; *plus* Doc Blake's own special ingredient—extract of foxberry, newest and most potent of the hallucinogenic potentiators."

Gregory was staring at his right hand, slowly clenching and unclenching it.

"The result," Blake went on, "is Doc Blake's total instantaneous many-splendored acid delight, guaranteed to make you hallucinate on the quarter-hour at least, or I return your money and give up my credentials as the best free-lance underground chemist ever to hit the West Village."

"You sound like you're stoned," Gregory said.

"Not at all," Blake protested. "I am merely on speed, just simple, old-fashioned amphetamines such as truck drivers and high school students swallow by the pound and shoot by the gallon. Speed is nothing more than a stimulant. With its assistance I can do my thing faster and better. My thing is to create my own quickie drug empire between Houston and 14th Street, and then bail out quickly, before I burn out my nerves or get crunched by the narcs or the Mafia, and *then* split for Switzerland where I will freak out in a splendid sanitorium surrounded by gaudy women, plump bank accounts, fast cars, and the respect of the local politicos."

Blake paused for a moment and rubbed his upper lip. "Speed *does* bring on a certain sense of grandiloquence, with accompanying verbosity . . . But never fear, my dear newly met friend and esteemed customer, my senses are more or less unimpaired and I am fully capable of acting as your guide for the superjumbotripout upon which you are now embarked."

"How long since I took that tablet?" Gregory asked.

Blake looked at his watch. "Over an hour ago."

"Shouldn't it be acting by now?"

"It should indeed. It undoubtedly is. *Something* should be happening."

Gregory looked around. He saw the grass-lined pit, the pulsing glowworm, the hard-packed mica, the captive cricket. He was on the side of the pit nearest to the drain pipe. Across from him, on the mossy gray stone, was Blake, his cilia matted and his exoderm mottled, poking at three speckled irregularly shaped tablets.

"What's the matter?" Blake asked.

Gregory scratched the tough membrane over his thorax. His cilia waved spasmodically in clear evidence of amazement, dismay, perhaps even fright. He extended a feeler, looked at it long and hard, bent it double and straightened it again.

Blake's antennae pointed straight up in a gesture of concern. "Hey, baby, speak to me! Are you hallucinating?"

Gregory made an indeterminate movement with his tail. "It started just before, when I asked you if I'd really have any hallucinations. I was into it then but I didn't realize it, everything seemed so natural, so ordinary . . . I was sitting on a *chair,* and you were on a *couch,* and we both had soft exoskeletons like—like mammals!"

"The shift into illusion is often imperceptible," Blake said. "One slides into them and out of them. What's happening now?"

Gregory coiled his segmented tail and relaxed his antennae. He looked around. The pit was dismayingly, tediously familiar. "Oh, I'm back to normal now. Do you think I'm going to have any more hallucinations?"

"Like I told you, I guarantee it," Blake said, neatly folding his glossy red wings and settling comfortably into a corner of the nest.

PAS DE TROIS OF THE CHEF AND THE WAITER AND THE CUSTOMER

Part One: The Chef

Dear God,
The incident which I want to speak to you about took place some years ago, when I opened the best Indonesian restaurant in the Balearic Islands.

I opened my restaurant in Santa Eulalia del Rio, which is a village on the island of Ibiza. At this time there already was an Indonesian restaurant in the port of Ibiza, and another in Palma de Mallorca. People have assured me that mine was easily the best.

Despite this, business was not good.

Santa Eulalia was very small, but there were numerous writers and artists living in the village and in the surrounding countryside. These people were all very poor; but not too poor to be unable to afford my rijstaffel. So why didn't they eat more often at my place? Surely it was not the competition from Juanito's Restaurant, or Sa Punta. Even granting those places full credit for their lobster mayonnaise and their paella, respectively, they could not approach my sambal telor, my sate kambing, and especially my babi ketjap.

I used to think the explanation lay in the fact that artists are nervous, temperamental people who need time to accustom themselves to new things, and especially to new restaurants.

I am that way myself, and I have been trying to become a painter for many years. That, in fact, is how I came to open my restaurant in a place like Santa Eulalia. I wanted to live near other artists, and to earn a living also.

Business was not good, but I was able to get by. My rent was low, I did my own cooking, and I had a local boy who served customers and changed records on the player and washed up the dishes afterwards. I didn't pay him much for all that, but only because I couldn't afford much. The boy was a marvel of a worker, always cheerful and clean, and with any luck he should someday become governor of the Balearics.

So I had my restaurant, which I called the Green Jade Moon, and I had my waiter, and within a week I had a steady customer.

I never did learn his name. He was a tall, thin, taciturn American with black hair. He might have been thirty or forty. He came in at nine o'clock every night and ordered the rijstaffel, ate it, paid, left a ten percent tip, and departed.

I exaggerate only slightly, for on Sundays he ate paella at Sa Punta, and on Tuesdays he ate the lobster mayonnaise at Juanito's. But why not, I ate in those places myself. The other five nights of the week he ate my rijstaffel, usually alone, once or twice with a woman, sometimes with a friend. He ate quietly, while Pablo, my waiter, bustled around serving dishes and changing records.

Frankly, I was able to live in Santa Eulalia off this customer alone. Not well, but I could live.

Prices were very cheap in those days.

Now of course, when you find yourself in a situation like that, when you more or less live from the spending of one customer, you tend to study that customer with some care.

That was the beginning of my sin. Like many sins, it seemed innocuous at first.

I wanted to encourage this man. I began to study what he liked and what he didn't like.

I served a thirteen-plate rijstaffel, charging 300 pesetas, which was then a little over five dollars. Rijstaffel means rice table. It is a Dutch adaption of Indonesian

Can You Feel Anything When I Do This? 127

cuisine. You put the rice in the center of the plate, and soak it with Sajor, a sort of vegetable soup. Then you surround the rice with various dishes—Daging Kerry, which is beef in curry sauce, and Sate Babi, roasted pork on skewers in peanut sauce, and Sambal Udang, liver in chili sauce. These are the expensive dishes, since they contain meat. Then there are Sambal Telor and Perkedel, eggs in chili sauce and meatballs, and various vegetable and fruit dishes. Finally there are the garnishes, like peanuts, shrimp wafers, grated coconut, spiced potato chips, and the like.

Everything is served in little oval plates, and it looks as if you are getting a great deal of food for your 300 pesetas. You are, of course, but not as much as it looks.

My customer ate with a good appetite, and he usually finished eight or ten of the dishes, plus a little over half the rice. That is good going for anyone who is not a Dutchman.

But I was not content with this. I noticed that he never ate liver. So I took it upon myself to substitute Sambal Ati, shrimps in liver sauce. He seemed especially to like my sates, and so I increased the amount, and gave him plenty of peanut sauce.

Within a week I could see that he was definitely gaining weight.

That encouraged me. I doubled his portion of Rempejek, peanut wafers, also the meatballs. The American began to eat like a Dutchman. He was filling out rapidly, and I was helping him along.

In two months he was some ten or twenty pounds overweight. I didn't care, I was trying to make him a prisoner of my food. I bought a set of larger plates and served him larger portions. I began to slip in another meat dish, Babi Ketjap, pork in soy sauce, in place of the peanuts he never touched.

By the third month he was trembling on the frontier of obesity. It was mainly the rice and the peanut sauce that did it to him. And I sat back in my kitchen and played on his tastebuds like an organist plays on an organ, and he dug in, his face round now and shining with sweat, while

Pablo gyrated around with the dishes and changed records like a dervish.

It was evident now, the man was susceptible to my rijstaffel. His Achilles heel was in his stomach, so to speak. But it was not even as simple as that. I had to assume that this American had lived his thirty or forty years prior to meeting me as a thin man. But what permits a man to remain thin? An omission, I think, a lack of some food that really engages the specific desires of his taste buds.

It is my own theory that many thin people are potentially fat people who simply have not found their appropriate and specific food. I once knew an emaciated German who only put on weight when he went to Madras for a construction firm and encountered the astounding spectrum of southern Indian curries. I knew a cadaverous Mexican working as a guitarist in various London night clubs, who assured me that he always gained weight in the city of his birth, Morelia. He told me that he could eat decently (though not voluptuously) anywhere in central Mexico; but that the cuisine from Oaxaca south to Yucatán, excellent though it was, was a total loss as far as he was concerned. And there was another man, an Englishman who had lived most of his life in China until the Communists expelled all foreigners, who assured me that he was wasting away for lack of Szechuanese food, and that Cantonese or Shanghai or Mandarin cooking did not suit him at all; he told me that the regional differences of cuisine in China are (or were) greater than those in Europe, and that his case was similar to that of a Neapolitan stranded in Stockholm. He told me that Szechuanese food was quite spicy, but delicate. He lived in Nice, on Provençal food, to which he added imported red bean curd and soy sauce and God knows what else. He told me it was a dog's life; but perhaps his wife was partly to blame for that.

There are precedents, you see, for the behavior of my American. He was evidently one of those men who have never encountered a cuisine which really suits them. He had found it now in my rijstaffel, and he was eating to make up for thirty or forty years of sensation-starvation.

Given a situation like this, the ethical chef must try to assume responsibility for his gluttonous customer. The chef, after all, is in the position of puppet-master; and it is he who manipulates the culinary desires of his customer. I have known a French chef in Paris, imbued with the spirit of Escoffier, who simply would not serve certain of his customers another portion of his Quiche Lorraine or his Tarte d'Ognon, two of his specialties, saying, "Seconds of anything are a distortion of a balanced meal, and I, for one, will not lend myself to the perpetration of perversities for a few lousy francs."

I applaud that master-chef, but I was unable to emulate him. I was not really a chef at all, simply a poor Italian with an unaccountable flair for preparing rijstaffel. My true desire was to be a painter. My character, much to my regret, was and still is opportunistic.

I continued to stuff my customer, and my anxieties tended to increase. It seemed to me that I owned the man now, although I had no legal bond. Late at night I would wake up trembling; I had dreamed that my customer had looked at me out of his enormous moon face and said, "Your sambals are lacking in savor. I was a fool ever to have allowed you to feed me. Our relationship is now at an end."

Recklessly I doubled his portions of Satay Kambing Madura, served his rice fried in oil and saffron rather than boiled, added a generous portion of Sate Ayam, chicken in chili sauce with ground nuts: all very fattening, all designed to maintain and increase his dependency on me.

It seems to me that I cooked, and he ate, in a state of delirium. Surely by this time neither of us were quite sane. He had become gross by this time, a distended sausage of a man. Each pound that he put on seemed to me a proof of my hold over him. But it was also a source of increased anxiety for me, for he could not keep on gaining weight forever.

And then, one night, it all changed.

I had planned a little additional delicacy for him, Sambal Ati, shrimps in chili sauce, a pure extravagance on my part when you consider the perpetually inflated cost of shrimps. Still, I thought he would enjoy it.

He did not come to the restaurant, even though it was one of his regular nights. I stayed open two hours later than usual, but he did not come.

The next night he did not come either.

On the third he did not come.

But on the fourth night he waddled in and took his accustomed table.

I had never spoken to the man in all the time he had eaten in my restaurant. But now I took the liberty of walking over to his table, bowing slightly, and saying, "We have missed you these past nights, mijnheer."

He said, "I was sorry that I was unable to come. But I was indisposed."

"Nothing serious, I trust?" I said.

"Certainly not. Merely a mild heart attack. But the doctor thought I should lie in bed a few days."

I bowed. He nodded. I returned to my kitchen. I poked at my serving pots. Pablo waited for me to ladle out the order. The American tucked the enormous red napkin I had bought specially for him into his collar and waited.

I became fully aware then of what I must have known all along: that I was killing this man.

I looked at my pots filled with sambals and sates, my caldrons of rice, my vats of Sajor, and I recognized them as instruments of slow death, as efficacious as a noose or a club.

Every man has his cuisine. But any man can be killed by the skillful manipulation of his appetites.

Suddenly I shouted to my customer, "The restaurant is closed!"

"But why?" he demanded.

"The meat has turned!" I replied.

"Then serve me a rijstaffel without meat," he replied.

"Impossible," I said. "There is no rijstaffel without meat."

He stared across the room at me, his eyes wide with alarm. "Then serve me an omelet made with plenty of butter."

"I do not make omelets."

"A pork chop then, with plenty of fat. Or just a bowl of fried rice."

"Mijnheer does not seem to understand," I told him. "I make only rijstaffel, properly and in the correct forms. When this becomes impossible, I make nothing at all."

"But I am hungry!" he cried like a plaintive child.

"Go eat lobster mayonnaise at Juanito's, or paella at Sa Punta. It wouldn't be the first time," I added, being only human.

"That's not what I want," he said, almost in tears. "I want rijstaffel!"

"Then go to Amsterdam!" I shouted at him, and kicked my pots of sates and sambals onto the floor and rushed out of the restaurant.

I packed a few belongings and caught a taxi to the city of Ibiza. I was in time to catch the night boat to Barcelona. From there I caught an airplane to Rome.

I had been cruel to my customer, I will grant that. But I thought it necessary. He had to be stopped at once from eating. And I had to be stopped from feeding him.

My further travels are not pertinent to this confession. I will only add that I now own and operate the finest rijstaffel restaurant on the Greek island of Cos. I get by. I serve mathematically exact portions, not a gram more even to my regulars. There is not enough money in the world to induce me to give or sell second helpings.

Thus I have learned a little virtue, but at the price of a great crime.

I have often wondered what happened to the American, and to Pablo, whose backwages I sent from Rome.

I am still trying to become a painter.

Part Two: The Waiter

Dear God,
My sin took place some years ago, when I worked as a waiter in an Indonesian restaurant in Santa Eulalia del

Rio, which is a villae in Ibiza, one of Spain's Balearic Islands.

I was young at the time, no more than eighteen. I had come to Ibiza as one of the crew of a French yacht. The owner had been caught smuggling American cigarettes, and his boat was impounded. The rest of the crew scattered. But I remained on Ibiza, coming at last to Santa Eulalia. I am Maltese, so I have a natural gift for languages. The villagers thought I was an Andalusian, and the foreign community thought I was an Ibicanco.

When the Dutchman opened his rijstaffel restaurant, I was uninterested at first. I helped him out for a day because I had nothing better to do, and because no one would work for the miserable wages he paid.

But in that first day I discovered his record collection.

This Dutchman had an extensive collection of 78s, some of them jazz classics. He had a good player, an adequate amplifier, and speakers which, in those days, were considered first-rate.

The man knew nothing about music, and cared less. He considered music a mere accompaniment to dining, an amenity, like candles in straw-covered bottles and strings of peppers and garlics on the wall. One played music while people ate: that was all he knew about it.

But I, Antonio Vargas, whom he called Pablo, I had a passion for music. Even at that young age I had already taught myself how to play the trumpet, guitar, and piano. What I lacked was an intimate knowledge of American jazz forms, which were my particular field of interest.

I saw at once that I could work for this Dutchman, perhaps earning enough to keep myself, and in the meantime play and replay his collection, learning the American musical idiom and preparing myself for the life of a musician.

The Dutchman was amenable to my playing the records. He had little choice, for who else would work for his wages? Certainly not the foreigners. Not even the native Ibicancos, who dress poorly but tend to be prosperous.

There was only me, and I considered myself well-paid by the Louis Armstrong alone.

Can You Feel Anything When I Do This? 133

I sorted and classified and dusted his records, forced him to order a needle with a diamond point from Barcelona, rearranged the locations of his speakers to avoid distortion, and worked out harmonious programs of jazz.

Frequently I would open with Duke Ellington's band playing "Mood Indigo"; reach Stan Kenton by the midpoint, and close by way of decompression, with Ella Fitzgerald singing "Bye-Bye Blues." But that was only one of my programs.

I soon noticed that I was playing to an audience of one not counting myself, and not counting the Dutchman, who couldn't tell Ravel from Ravi Shankar.

You see, I had acquired a listener. He was a tall, thin, taciturn Britisher, and demonstrably an aficionado of jazz. I saw that he ate in tempo with the music I played, slowly and lingeringly if I had on "You Ain't Been Blue," quickly and abruptly if I played "Caravan."

But more than that, his moods altered visibly as I changed records. Ellington and Kenton tended to elevate him, he would eat furiously, beating time with his left hand as he shoveled in the rijstaffel with his right. Charlie Barnet and Bird acted as depressants, no matter what their tempos, and his eating would slow down and he would purse his lips and knot his brows.

When you are a musician as myself, you wish to please your audience; always staying within your métier, of course. And I set out to capture my only listener.

I leaned heavily on Ellington and Kenton at first, because I was still unsure of myself. I could never accustom him to Charlie Parker's monumental fantasies, and Barnet seemed to grate on his nerves. But I educated him to Louis Armstrong, Ella Fitzgerald, Earl Hines, and the Modern Jazz Quartet. I was even able to pinpoint the individual sides he liked best, and to orchestrate an evening for him alone.

The Britisher was a stupendous listener. But he paid a price, of course: night after night he had to eat the Dutchman's rijstaffel, which was a collection of little stews with various names, all of them possessing the same overspiced taste of chili sauce. There was no getting around this; the

Dutchman did not encourage people to hang around without eating. When you walked in he stuck a menu in your hand. As you finished the last dish, he put the bill on your table. This may be acceptable practice in Amsterdam, but it is simply not done in Spain. Particularly the foreign community, which acted more Spanish than the Spaniards, disapproved, and stayed away. As a result of his crudeness and greed, the Dutchman could only rely on a single customer, the Englishman who really came to hear the records.

After a while I noticed that my listener was gaining weight. I accepted that as an accolade for my beloved jazz, and for me, the selector and orchestrator of that jazz. Anyone who could continue to plow through that monolithic and unspeakable rijstaffel was an aficionado indeed.

I was young, careless, irresponsible. I took no heed to my duties as a musician, viz., to provide balance and catharsis as well as fascination. No, I was out to capture this man, win him with my records, enslave him to Armstrong, Ellington, and myself.

The Englishman grew fat. I ought to have played something austere and classical, like Bix Beiderbecke or some of the other Dixieland formalists. They were not to his tastes, but they might have had a restraining effect upon him. But I did not. Shamelessly I gave him what he wanted.

What is worse, I perverted my own taste to please him. One evening I spun Glenn Miller's "String of Pearls," an amiable piece with no great pretensions. I did it as a sort of musical joke. But I saw at once that the Englishman had a taste for big-hand swing.

I should have simply ignored it, of course. The man had talent as a listener, but he was musically uneducated. Had I been willing to take the gamble, I might have taught him something important, might have demonstrated to him what music is really about.

But I did no such thing. Instead, I catered shamelessly to his sentimental passion. I played Glenn Miller, Tommy Dorsey, Harry James. I covered myself esthetically by spinning Benny Goodman; but I sunk to the depths by brazenly spinning Vaughan Monroe.

It is a terrible thing to have such power over another person. Within months, I could program my listener as well as my records.

When he came in I might toy with him slightly, playing "Muskrat Ramble," a composition beyond his comprehension. Then abruptly I would turn to Vaughn Monroe's "Moon Over Miami," and the Englishman's frown would depart, a slight smile would touch his gross lips, and he would shovel away at the unpalatable rijstaffel.

The chef, in his vanity, loaded up the man's plates. But it was I who made him eat.

Sometimes, when I was playing "Take the A Train," for example, or Armstrong's "Beale Street Blues," the Englishman would sigh petulantly, put down his fork, seem incapable of eating any more. Then I would quickly put on Glenn Miller's "String of Pearls," or his "Blue Evening," or "Pink Cocktail for a Blue Lady." Or I would hit him with Harry James's "When You're a Long, Long Way from Home," or Jimmy Dorsey's "Amapola."

These frivolities acted upon him like a drug. His bullet head nodding in time, tears forming in his eyes, he would dig in with his soup spoon.

He grew monstrous, and I continued to manipulate him like a trained rat. I don't know where it might have all ended.

Then one night he didn't show up.

He didn't come the next night either, or the one after that.

On the fourth night he came to the restaurant, and the chef (understandably worried about his main source of income), inquired about his health.

The man replied that he had had an ulcer attack, had been ordered to stay on bland foods for a few days, but was now feeling fit again.

The chef nodded and went back to dish up his fiery stews.

The Englishman looked at me and addressed me for the first time. I remember that I was playing Stan Kenton's "Down in an Alley by the Alamo" at the time. The Englishman said, "Forgive my asking this, but might you be so good as to play Vaughn Monroe's 'Moon Over Miami'?"

"Of course, my pleasure," I replied, and walked back to the player. I took off the Kenton side. I picked up the Monroe. And I realized then that I was killing this man, literally killing him.

He had become addicted to my records. The only way he could hear them was by eating rijstaffel, which was making holes in his stomach.

At that moment I grew up.

"No more Vaughn Monroe!" I shouted suddenly.

He blinked his great saucer eyes in bewilderment. The chef came out of his kitchen, amazed that I had raised my voice.

The Englishman said, in a pleading voice, "Perhaps a little Glenn Miller . . ."

"No more of that," I told him.

"Tommy Dorsey?"

"Out of the question."

The unfortunate man was trembling, and his great jowls were beginning to quiver. He said, "Duke Ellington, then."

"No!"

The chef said, "But Pablo, you *like* Duke Ellington!"

The customer said, "Or play Beiderbecke, or even the Modern Jazz Quartet! Play what you like, but play!"

"You've had too much," I told him, "As far as I'm concerned, the music is finished."

I brought my fist down on the amplifier, shattering various tubes.

The chef and the customer were speechless.

I walked out, not bothering to ask for my two weeks' back wages. I hitchhiked into the port of Ibiza and took deck passage on a ship to Marseilles.

Today I am a saxophone player of some renown, and can be heard every night except Sunday at Le Cat's Pajamas Club on the Rue de Hachette in Paris. I am admired for my classical purity and form, and I am respected as a purist of Dixieland Jazz.

But I still have this sin upon my head, of hypnotizing and stuffing that poor Englishman by giving him the music he desired.

I regret it most sincerely.

I have often wondered since then what happened to the chef and to the customer.

Part Three: The Customer

Dear God,

My sin took place many years ago, in a little Spanish town called Santa Eulalia del Rio. I have never before acknowledged this sin: but now I feel impelled to do so.

I had gone to Santa Eulalia to write a book. My wife had gone with me. We had no children.

While I was there, a man opened up a rijstaffel restaurant. I think that the man was a Finn or possibly a Hungarian. His restaurant was welcomed by all the expatriate colony. Before this man came, we had our choice of eating paella at Sa Punta or lobster mayonnaise at Juanito's. The food was fine in both places, but after a while even the best of dishes become monotonous.

Many of us began to eat at the Yin-Tang, as he called it. Things were always lively there. Add to that the fact that the Hungarian had a fine collection of records and a more than adequate sound system. A place like that could not fail.

I began to eat there about five nights a week. My wife was a lovely woman, but not much of a cook. I was one of the Hungarian's regular customers.

After about a week, I took notice of the waiter.

He was young, no more than sixteen or seventeen, and I think he was an Indonesian. He had coloring of the purest shade of olive oil, and his hair and eyebrows were sooty black. He was slender, graceful, quick. It was a pleasure to watch him darting around, serving dishes and changing records.

Harmless-sounding, isn't it? But what ensued was a darker, less innocent complication.

As I said, I admired his grace and beauty, as one man may admire the attributes of another man. But by the second week, I found myself taking special notice of the tender lines of his cheek, the proud lift of his head, the set of his shoulders and back, and the exquisite curve of his buttocks.

I entered into a state of self-deception. I told myself that I was admiring the boy much as one would admire Greek statuary, or the heroic figures of Michelangelo. I told myself that my interest was esthetic, and nothing more. And I continued to go to the restaurant almost every night, and to eat rijstaffel, which is one of the most fattening cuisines on earth.

By the end of the month I realized, with terrible dismay, that I was infatuated with the boy. I became aware that I wished to touch him, stroke his hair, trace the lines of his body, and do other, even more awful things.

I have never been a homosexual. I have never had any reason to consider myself a potential homosexual. I have always enjoyed sexual relations with women, and have never been able to understand how any man could enjoy the body of any other man.

Now I knew, to my regret.

I was spared the shame of my realization only because of the immensity of my obsession. Every night I went to the restaurant, and stayed for as long as I decently could. The chef took to giving me extra portions, and I ate them, grateful for an excuse to remain longer.

And the boy? I cannot think that he was unconscious of my thoughts. I cannot think that he did not reciprocate. For, as the days and months passed, he hurled himself around the restaurant in a veritable frenzy, changing records, emptying already clean ashtrays, displaying himself in a rather shameless manner.

Often we exchanged meaningful looks, the boy and I. At this point my wife had gone back to the United States. The chef was oblivious to anything but the consumption of rijstaffel. And the boy and I eyed each other, made our intentions clear, but never exchanged a word or a touch.

I gained weight, of course. Who could pack away two

or three pounds of rijstaffel a night and not gain weight? I gained weight insensibly, caught up in my obsession, and in my self-loathing. I neglected my friends, paid no attention to my appearance. I would leave the restaurant each night, my stomach groaning at the mass of overspiced food within it. I would go to bed and dream of the boy, and wait impatiently for the next night when I could see him again.

Our looks became bolder, more brazen. Sometimes, when he served the dishes, he would rest his hand upon the table, as if daring me to touch it. And I would clear my throat, my eyes reproaching him for being a shameless flirt.

Swept up in this madness, I do not know how long things might have gone on, or where they might have gone to. I was losing my shyness, losing my pride, I was coming close to speaking to the boy outright. Then, quite unexpectedly, I noticed something.

I noticed that I was the only customer that the restaurant had left.

I thought about this, I pondered it deeply. I had dropped my friends over the last months, or they had dropped me. Still, why had they stopped eating at the rijstaffel restaurant?

I went night after night, and it was the same, I was the only customer. Yet I could detect no loss of quality in the food, or in the music. Everything was the same; except for me.

I saw something then. It came to me on one night much like all other nights, when I was plowing through the usual tremendous servings. I saw that I had grown monstrously fat over the course of several months. And for a moment I viewed myself from the outside:

I saw a disgustingly gross man seated in a small restaurant. A man fat enough to turn your stomach. A man in whose company you would not want to eat.

It came to me then: *I* was the reason why the Hungarian had lost all of his customers. For what man in his right mind would want to eat with me there? And I was there all of the time.

An insight like that must he acted upon immediately, or lost forever. I pushed the table away and got to my feet, not without some difficulty. The chef and the waiter stared at me. I began to waddle toward the door.

The chef cried, "Is something the matter with the food?"

"Not with the food," I replied, "with me."

The boy said with downcast eyes, "Perhaps I have offended you . . ."

"Quite the contrary," I replied, "you have pleased me immensely, but I have offended myself beyond measure."

They didn't understand. The chef cried out, "Won't you at least eat a plate of pork sate, just made, fresh and delicious?"

And the boy said, "There's a new Armstrong record which you have not heard yet."

I stopped at the door. I said, "Thank you both very much. You are kind people. But I happen to be destroying myself here under your very eyes. I shall go away now and complete that task by myself."

They stared at me, wild-eyed and uncomprehending. I waddled out of the restaurant, to my apartment, packed a light suitcase, and found a taxi to take me into Ibiza city. I was just in time for the night flight to Barcelona.

Years have passed since that time. Time and distance stripped away my obsession. I have been in love since then, but never again with a boy.

I live now in San Miguel de Allende, in Mexico, with my wife (not the same one I came to Santa Eulalia with) and our two children.

I have often wondered what happened to the chef and the waiter. Presumably they continued their business, prospered. They may still be in Santa Eulalia, for all I know. Unless, of course, my lustful sin destroyed them in some way.

I regret my sin sincerely.

I am still trying to become a writer.

ASPECTS OF LANGRANAK

1

I can't describe this place without describing me. Nor can I describe me without telling you about the place. But which should I start with? Perhaps I ought to describe both of us together. But I doubt if I could manage that. Perhaps I am incapable of describing anything.

Still, I *am* on an alien planet—a situation which is commonly considered interesting. And I am an individual, which is also supposed to be interesting. And I am certainly capable of writing down my impressions. I don't know why I can't bring it all together.

Perhaps I should start with a description of my inability to describe anything. But I seen to have done that, for whatever it's worth.

2

I think I will start with the spires.

The main city here is called Langranak. It is notable for its spires. From the vantage-point of a hill some five miles outside of the city, the aspect is one of a multiplicity of spires. They are all shapes and sizes and colors. I have been told that Venice also has many spires, and Istanbul as well. Spires present a pleasing esthetic pattern, no matter what their arrangement. The spires of Langranak present a definitely alien aspect. I think that is all I have to say about spires.

3

I am an individual from Earth of average size and

shape. I suppose I am like a lot of people. I am unusual in that I am on an alien planet.

I spend most of my time inside the spaceship. Great pains were taken to make this spaceship homelike and cozy. The main lounge looks like a Holiday Inn. The galley is reminiscent of a Howard Johnson's, and the bedroom might have been taken from a New England country inn. I feel pretty good in this spaceship. I used to laugh at American décor, but I don't any longer. I like my spaceship very much just as it is. I like the pizza dispensing machine and the Coca-Cola fountain. The hot dogs are from Nathan's. Only the hot buttered corn on the cob is not up to Earth standards. They still haven't licked that problem.

4

Nothing much happens here. That is the part I wanted to avoid mentioning. My idea of a story is that it should have adventure and conflict and problems and resolutions. That's the kind of story I like to read. But nothing much happens to me. Here I am on an alien planet surrounded by alien beings, and nothing much happens to me. Nevertheless, I still believe I have a story here. Christ knows, I have all of the ingredients.

5

Yesterday I had an interview with the chief magistrate of Langranak. We discussed transspatial friendship. We both agreed that our races ought to be friends. We also talked about interstellar trade, which we both agreed upon in principle. But in fact, there doesn't seem to be much that we have that they want, and vice-versa. Not enough to justify the high freighting costs. I mean, they have a whole planet in which to manufacture what they need, and so do we. So we had to merely agree in principle.

We made more progress when we talked about a tourist interchange program. These people like to travel, and so do our people. The costs would be extremely high, but some people could afford it. Anyhow, it would be a beginning.

6

I sit in my spaceship and do a lot of reading. I read many books on Zen Buddhism, and also on Yoga and on Tibetan and Hindu mysticism. "Enter the silence as often as possible, stay in it as long as possible." That's what it's all about, really. Methods of stopping your mind from chattering. "One-pointedness." I want all of that very much, but my mind refuses to stay still. I have random thoughts, emotions, sensations. Sometimes I can control all of that for five minutes at a time. But that doesn't give me much of a feeling of accomplishment. I suppose I need a guru. But that is impossible due to my circumstances. I thought about making inquiries here for a teacher. But I won't be here long enough to make it worthwhile. It always seems to be that way.

7

Nothing seems very strange here, really. People buy things and sell things. They work at various jobs. There are a few beggars. It all seems quite comprehensible. I don't understand everything, of course; but I don't understand everything at home, either. I wish I could say, "What these people do about this is simply incredible." But nothing strikes me as especially incredible. They go about their work and live their lives, and I do the same, and it all seems pretty normal. I have to keep on reminding myself that I am on an alien planet. Not that I can ever forget it, of course. It's just that I can't seem to get into the sense of wonder.

8

Last night there was an eclipse. I had planned to go out and see it but fell asleep over a book and missed the whole thing. Not that it matters. The ship's cameras recorded it automatically and I'll catch it on replay.

9

I pulled myself together today and went out to visit the ruins. People have been urging me to see them. I am very glad that I went. The ruins, which are believed to be of a civilization some thousands of years vanished, are situated approximately ten miles from the outskirts of Langranak. They are very extensive. I looked at three large temples, partially reconstructed. They were covered with intricate carving and bas-relief figures of various creatures which my guide told me do not literally exist. There also were statues, quite grotesque and stylized. The guide said that these had once been worshiped as gods, but were no longer. There were also several labyrinths which once had a religious significance.

I took photographs of all of these things. Light conditions were average. I used a Nikon with a 50-mm. lens, occasionally switching to a 90-mm. lens.

Late in the day my guide pointed out the interesting fact that nowhere in all the intricate carvings was there any use of the parallelogram. The builders of these ruins may have considered the parallelogram to be esthetically unpleasing or religiously taboo. It is also conceivable that they simply had not discovered the parallelogram shape, although they made extensive use of the square and the rectangle. No one knows for sure.

Investigation is still going on. Clarification of this point should throw a great deal of light on the psychology of this ancient and mysterious people.

10

Holiday today. I went into the city and sat at one of the cafes and drank what passes for coffee around here and watched people pass. It was a very colorful spectacle. According to the brochure, this holiday is in celebration of an important military victory over a neighboring country. The two countries now seem to be on good terms, or at least fair terms. But it is hard to be sure about things like that.

11

There are three important and distinct racial stocks living in this city. The older inhabitants look like Englishmen, the older immigrants look like Frenchmen, and the newer immigrants look like Turks. There are various tensions between these groups. Regional dress, once prominent here, has died out except for special holidays. Everybody regrets the passing of the old customs.

12

Sometimes, in the evening, I get sad and homesick. On those nights I can't get to sleep. I read and listen to tapes. I watch a movie on the ship's projector. Then I take a sleeping pill. A couple of pills, actually. I think it's because I'm homesick. But then I remember that I used to feel the same way at home. I used sleeping pills at home too.

13

I'm afraid that this is not a very interesting planet. People tell me it's more interesting in the other hemisphere. But I don't think I'll go there. The friendship treaty is signed now and my work is done. I guess I'll be taking off. I'm sorry this wasn't a more exotic place. But I hope to do better in my next exploration.

PLAGUE CIRCUIT

Inexperienced travelers usually try to materialize in perfect concealment. They come stumbling out of broom closets, storerooms, phone booths, or whatever else the situation affords, hoping desperately that they've made a smooth transition. And inevitably, such behavior only calls attention to them—the very thing they wanted to avoid. But for a seasoned traveler like me, the thing was simple. My destination was the New York of August 1988. I chose the evening rush hour, and materialized in the middle of a Times Square crowd.

It calls for a certain knack, of course. You can't just *appear*. You have to be moving as soon as you materialize, head slightly bent and shoulders hunched, a glassy look in your eye. That way, no one notices you.

I made it perfectly, suitcase in hand, and hurried into a downtown local. I exited in Sheridan Square and walked to Washington Square Park.

The location I picked for myself was near a large cistern not far from the Washington Square arch. I set down my suitcase and clapped my hands together briskly. Several people looked at me. I chanted, "Gather around, friends, gather around and hear the opportunity of a lifetime. Don't be bashful, step up and hear the good news."

A small crowd began to form. A young man called out, "Hey, whatcha selling?" I smiled at him but did not answer. I wasn't going into my pitch until I had a fair-sized audience.

I continued my patter. "Come close, friends, come close and hear the big news. This is what you've been waiting for, friends, the great opportunity, the last chance! Don't let it pass you by!"

Can You Feel Anything When I Do This? 147

Soon I had collected about thirty people. I decided that was enough for a start.

"Good citizens of New York," I said. "I wish to speak to you about the strange disease which has suddenly come into your lives, the epidemic popularly called the Blue Plague. All of you must know by now that there is no cure for this wholesale killer. I realize that your doctors continue to assure you that research is progressing, that a breakthrough can be expected momentarily, that a method of treatment will infallibly be discovered soon. But the fact is, they have found no serum, no antibody, no specific whatsoever for the Blue Plague. How could they? They have not been able to discover the cause of the disease, much less how to stop it. To date all they have produced are unworkable and contradictory theories. Due to the rapid spread, extreme virulence and unknown properties of the disease, we must anticipate that the doctors will be unable to produce a cure in time to assist you, the afflicted. You must expect what has been true of all epidemics throughout the recorded history of the world: that despite all attempts at treatment and control, the disease will continue to rage unchecked until it has exhausted itself or run out of victims."

Someone in the crowd laughed, and several people were grinning. I put this down to hysteria, and went on.

"What is to be done, then? Are you to remain the passive victims of the plague, seduced into quietness by people who will not reveal to you the true state of hopelessness? Or will you consent to try something new, something that comes without the seal of approval of a discredited politico-medical authority?"

By now I had a crowd of about fifty people. Quickly I ended my pitch.

"Your doctors can't protect you from the Blue Plague, my friends, but I can!"

Quickly I opened my suitcase and took out a handful of large yellow capsules.

"This is the drug that will conquer the Blue Plague, my friends. There is no time to explain how I came by it, or how it works. Nor will I engage in scientific double-talk. But I will give concrete proof instead."

The crowd became silent and attentive. Now I knew that I had them.

"As proof," I shouted, "bring me a diseased person. Bring me ten! If there is still life in them, I undertake to cure them within seconds of their swallowing this capsule! Bring them up here, friends! I will cure any man, woman, or child suffering from the Blue Plague!"

The silence held for a second more; then the crowd broke into laughter and applause. Astonished, I listened to the comments on all sides of me.

"College stunt?"

"He's kinda old to be a hippy."

"I bet he's doing it for some TV show."

"Hey, mister, what's the gag?"

I was too shocked to attempt an answer. I simply stood there with my suitcase at my feet and the capsules in my hand. I hadn't made a single sale in this plague city! I couldn't even give my drugs away! It was unthinkable. The crowd dispersed, all except for one girl.

"What kind of a stunt is this?" she asked me.

"Stunt?"

"It's a publicity stunt of some kind, isn't it? Are you opening a restaurant or a boutique? Tell me about it. Maybe I can arrange some coverage."

I put the handful of capsules into my jacket pocket. The girl said, "Look, I work on a Village newspaper. We go for weird put-ons. Tell me about it."

She was quite a pretty girl. I judged her to be in her mid-twenties, slender, brown-haired and brown-eyed. Her self-confidence struck me as pathetic.

"This is no trick," I told her. "If you people haven't the sense to take precautions against the plague—"

"What plague?" she asked me.

"The Blue Plague. The plague that's sweeping through New York."

"Look, pal," she said, "there's no plague in New York, not blue, black, yellow, or any other kind. Now just what is this stunt of yours, really?"

Can You Feel Anything When I Do This? 149

"No plague?" I asked her. "Are you sure?"

"I'm positive."

"Perhaps they're concealing it from the people," I said. "Though that would be difficult. Five to ten thousand deaths a day couldn't be kept out of the newspapers . . . This is August 1988, isn't it?"

"Yes. Hey," she said, "you look a little pale. Are you feeling all right?"

"I'm fine," I said, although I wasn't.

"Maybe you'd better sit down."

She walked with me to a park bench. It had suddenly struck me that perhaps I had gotten the year wrong. Perhaps the company had actually meant 1990 or 1998. If that was true, I had cost them a good deal in time-travel fees, and had possibly invalidated my peddler's license by trying to sell drugs in a non-disaster area.

I took out my wallet and removed the small pamphlet entitled *The Plague Circuit*. This pamphlet lists all the great plague years, type of plague, percentage of population killed, and other pertinent data. With considerable relief I saw that I was in the right place at the right time. New York, in August of 1988, was supposed to be deep in the Blue Plague.

"*The Plague Circuit?*" she asked, reading over my shoulder. "What is that?"

I should have moved away from her. I should even have dematerialized. The company has strict rules about salesmen giving out anything but the information we're taught to give out in the training course. But now I didn't care. Suddenly I wanted to talk to this pretty bright-haired girl in her quaint clothing, sitting in the sunshine with me in a doomed city.

"*The Plague Circuit*," I said, "is a list of the years and places that have had major plagues, or will have them. Like the Great Plague at Constantinople in 1346, or the London Plague of 1664."

"I suppose you were at those?"

"Yes. I was sent by my company, Temporal Medical Services. Among other things, we're licensed to sell drugs in disaster areas."

"Then you're from some place in the future where they have time travel?"

"Yes."

"That's wonderful," she said. "You go around peddling pills in disaster areas. Really, you don't look like the sort of person who makes a living out of other people's misery."

She didn't know the half of it, and I wasn't going to tell her. "It's necessary work," I said.

"Anyhow," she said, "you've overlooked the fact that there's no plague here."

"Something must have gone wrong," I said. "I have an advance man who's supposed to scout these things out for me."

"Maybe he got lost in the time stream or something."

She was enjoying herself. For my part I found the whole thing ghastly. This girl, unless she was one of the fortunate few, would not survive the plague. But I also found it fascinating to talk to her. This was the first time I had ever had a conversation with a plague victim.

She said, "Well, it's been nice talking to you. Frankly, I don't know if I can use your story."

"I'd prefer you didn't." I took a handful of capsules from my pocket. "Please take these."

"Oh really now—"

"I'm serious. They're for you and your family. Please keep them. They'll be useful, you'll see."

"All right, thank you very much. Happy time-traveling."

I watched her walk away. As she turned a corner I thought I saw her drop the capsules. But I couldn't be sure.

I sat down on a park bench and waited.

It was close to midnight before George came. Furiously I said, "What happened? I made a damned fool of myself. There isn't any plague here!"

"Take it easy," George said. "I had expected to be here a week ago, but the company got a government directive to cancel everything for one year. Then they were told to cancel the cancellation and proceed as planned."

"Why didn't anyone tell me about the delay?" I asked.

"You should have been notified. But everything became confused. I really am sorry. But we can begin now."

"Do we really have to?" I asked.

"Have to what?"

"You know," I said.

He stared at me. "What's the matter with you? You weren't like this in London."

"But that was in 1664. This is 1988. It's closer to our own time. And these people seem more—human."

"I hope you haven't been fraternizing," George said.

"Of course not!"

"All right," George said. "I know that this work can get emotionally distasteful. But you have to take a realistic view. The Census Board gave them plenty of chances. It gave them the hydrogen bomb."

"Yes."

"But they didn't use it on each other. And the Board gave them all the means for a really big bacteriological war, but they didn't use that, either. And the Board also gave them all the information they needed to curb population growth voluntarily. But they couldn't bring themselves to use any of it. They just continued their indiscriminate breeding, crowding out the other species and each other, poisoning and depleting the Earth—just as they always do."

I knew all of this, but it helped me to hear it again.

"Nothing can grow indefinitely," George went on. "All living things must be subject to control. For most species, check and balance do the job mechanically. But human beings have gone beyond natural restraints. They have to do the job for themselves. If they can't or won't, then somebody has to do it for them."

Suddenly George looked tired and troubled. "But humans never see the necessity of thinning themselves out," he said. "They never learn. That's why our plagues are necessary."

"All right," I said, "let's get on with it."

"About twenty percent of them will survive this one," George said. I think he was trying to reassure himself.

He took a flat silver flask out of his pocket. He unstopped it. He walked over and poured its contents into a sewer. sewer.

"That's that. You can start selling your pills within a week. After that, our schedule calls for stops in London, Paris, Rome, Istanbul, Bombay, and so on."

I nodded. It had to be done. But sometimes it's tough to be a gardener of people.

TAILPIPE TO DISASTER

When he heard the news, Chief Pilot Johnny Draxton's reaction was instantaneous. "What?" he bellowed. "Me fly with some green kid just out of the Space Academy as my co-pilot?"

Big, tough, grizzled Sergeant Rack nodded in wry sympathy. "Maybe it won't be so bad, sir. These young kids have been raised on the interstellar ships. They ain't like us old interplanetary men."

"Yeah?" Draxton sneered, clamping his strong jaws on half an inch of well-chewed cigar. "You think a green kid can co-pilot a double warp-powered GP-1077F2 interstellar attack bomber armed with a full rack of XX fusion bombs in spatial area 12BAA where a single mistake can mean instant death? Who is this kid?"

"General Deverell's son, sir," the tough, grizzled old sergeant said.

Johnny Draxton smiled grimly and spat out the well-chewed end of his cigar. "So the general thinks he can shove his kid into a GP-1077F2, huh? Well, Sarge, we'll just see about that."

Draxton's smile was ominous. He crushed his ancient flight cap over his eyes and swung out of Operations ProComSubShack, a lithe, pantherlike figure.

Sergeant Rack shook his head wryly. He had been afraid of something like this. Men like Johnny Draxton had a natural prejudice against general's sons. Johnny had come up the hard way. In the war-torn skies over Mierdolan V, Johnny Draxton's single-seater tractor-power Invictus Mk.-2 had helped rid the galaxy of Kalnakak ships; and Johnny had helped, too. Between wars, Johnny had stayed in practice by shooting down commercial spacecraft on the Luna-Mars run. "Preparedness," he often told his friends, "is worth any price." Johnny was a real tiger of space, aggressive, fierce, scornful, cigar-smoking.

And the general's son? Well, maybe it would be all right, thought the tough, wry, but ever-hopeful Sergeant Rack. But trouble came sooner than even he, always prepared for trouble, had expected.

It happened on the first flight. The general's son, whose name was Hubert Deverell, had been introduced to the crew. He had shaken hands with taciturn Bombardier Bluefeather, a full-blooded Apache Indian; with Chief Gunner Ash, a wisecracking, intense boy from Brooklyn; and with Milton St. Augustus Lee, a soft-spoken engineer from Alabama. Deverell was a big lad with deceptively slow movements, his blond hair cropped close to his skull, his gray eyes intense, his lieutenant's bars glistening. He had gone forward to the pilot's compartment to pay his respects.

"I just wanted to say, sir," the general's son blurted, "that it's a great pleasure to serve with you. I—I've always admired your record, sir."

Johnny's eyes, the color of raw Irish whiskey before distilling, gave no hint of his feelings. "Glad to have you on board, Deverell," he said, and Sergeant Rack began to feel that the conflict, and thus the rest of this story, could be averted.

But such was not the case. The young lieutenant blurted, "You see, sir, I've always wanted to be a part of an interstellar attack bomber ship crew. My father says they—they're *important!*"

"I'm glad to hear General Deverell's opinion," Johnny said coolly. "It may interest you to know Lieutenant, that you are leaning against the tail assembly release toggle."

"Gosh!" the kid said, and moved away from the panel with deceptive awkwardness.

"It wasn't armed, of course," Johnny said. "But a few little mistakes like that when we're out in enemy space—"

"I'll be careful, sir!" Lieutenant Deverell said. "Yes,

Can You Feel Anything When I Do This? 155

sir," he added with pathetic willingness to please, "I'll surely be careful, sir."

Johnny Draxton only smiled grimly. Sergeant Rack put out a kindly hand the size and color of a Kashmiri saddle, and took the young lieutenant by the shoulder.

"Come with me, sir," he said. "I'll show you around."

In front of them, the huge hemispheric control board glittered and danced like a drunken IBM machine. And Johnny Draxton, his strong jaws clamped on a fresh but rapidly wilting cigar, looked amused.

Eighty-seven hours later, the hugh attack-bomber was hurtling through sector 12BAA on a routine patrol mission. Below them, the disputed planet Mnos II glowed an ominous red-brown, its major continent sprawled like an upside-down dragon with its teeth pulled. Draxton cracked the pulsors and the big ship wailed; he hit the boosters and the big ship screamed; he slammed in the forward tractors and the big ship moaned.

"OK, kid," Johnny said to the fresh-faced big-handed lieutenant, "you take her now."

The general's son climbed clumsily into the co-pilot's seat and nervously strapped the duo-webbing around his big chest. He reached forward and took a grip on the side-panel retractor control nozzle with one hand, the other resting on the ring pin retaining gear assembly.

"Take her through an XBX maneuver," Johnny said. "And watch yourself. We're carrying live eggs this trip."

The kid gulped, nodded, and swallowed. Under his thick, deft fingers the dials spun and danced, and the huge interstellar ship nosed upward. Deverell cracked the throttles, and the patrol-bomber whimpered. The kid grinned and punched the level-out.

"Deverell!" Draxton shouted.

"Sir?"

"That was the bomb release you punched. Congratulations. You have just dropped a stick of XX fusion busters onto a nominally neutral planet."

The kid turned sickly white under his tan. Johnny

added, "Anyhow, you would have dropped them if the bomb-release hadn't been interlocked. What in hell is the matter with you?"

"I guess it's taking me a little while getting used to things," the kid said, nervousness but no fear showing in his clumsy voice.

"Yeah?" Johnny said, and chewed his cigar down to half an inch. "Nervous, huh? Well, let's see you take her through a series JB2 multiple diminishing radius turn."

"Captain!" Sergeant Rack cried, concern showing on his wry, leathery face. "That could peel the hide right off her!"

"We might have to do it in combat sometime," Draxton said. "Go ahead, Deverell."

The kid gulped, swallowed, and gripped the controls in a shaking hand. The big interstellar attack-bomber began to nose inexorably up and over . . .

Back in the crew's section, Bombardier Bluefeather was writing a letter to his mother, a full-blooded Apache. Repeatedly he wet the end of the pencil with his narrow tongue, and wrote, "I hope the corn is coming up green on the reservation this year."

Gunner Ash was thinking about Flatbush Extension. Although he was an intense, wisecracking type, he found that he missed the old street. And he missed Kitty Callahan, his wife of only three hours.

Milton St. Augustus Lee, the soft-spoken and deceptively quiet Southerner, was thinking of his wife Amelia, who, right now, was probably drinking coffee with Lieutenant Deverell's bright, soft-eyed fiancée, Faye. They were swell kids, all of them. For a moment St. Augustus Lee could forget his bitter anger about the War between the States. Hell . . . Some Yankees weren't so bad . . .

As the big attack-bomber came out of its first roll, a shudder passed through ship, throwing Ash and Lee out of their bunks. Bluefeather, with a taciturn ease born of centuries on horseback, grabbed a stanchion retainer rod. The spaceship whipped over onto its back and began to fall like a rock.

"What the hell?" Ash asked. No one answered the wisecracking Brooklyn boy.

Up forward in the pilot's compartment, young Lieutenant Deverell had missed the triple-thrust breakout button and hit instead the fallaway accelerometer, which was not interlocked. It was an easy enough error to correct; but Deverell's hands were locked to the controls in the unmistakable signs of panic. Sergeant Rack, that ancient and indestructible judger of young pilots, had seen it happen often enough. Without anger he clubbed the young lieutenant across the jaw with a fist the size and color of a Kashmiri saddle. Deverell slumped back in his seat, and Johnny Draxton pulled the ship out of the deadly spin.

"Well now," Draxton said coolly, "I reckon that takes care of the kid's career as a pilot."

"Don't be too hard on him, sir," Rack said, as the boy shook his head groggily. "It happens to the best of them. Seems to me I remember your first mission, sir, when you—"

"Shaddap!" Draxton roared, his tiger's face going livid with anger. "You heard me, Sergeant. This kid's washed up."

They had all heard him, since the young lieutenant, in falling back against the control panel, had inadvertently turned on the intership intercom interrelay system. The Indian, breaking his habitual silence, exhaled air through his nostrils. St. Augustus Lee said, "That's rather a tough break for the boy. I wonder if . . ." He didn't finish. Gunner Ash said, "What the hell?" But no one laughed. It was too serious for wisecracks.

Up front, young Lieutenant Deverell thought of his father, tall and ramrod-straight, gray-haired, thin-lipped, long-fingered, with the look of cold-rolled magnesium steel in his bleak gray general's eyes. He thought of his fiancée, bright, soft-eyed Faye with her coffee and her high hopes. He thought of the Space Academy, the flag, the anthem; he thought of San Francisco, a place he had always wanted to see. And he knew that somehow he must atone.

Johnny Draxton sat full square in front of the glittering switchboard, his cigar chewed down to a quarter of an inch, his tiger's smile upon his face.

And for the first time in his life, young Lieutenant Deverell knew anger.

Suddenly the huge attack-bomber shook as though in pain. Simultaneously Ash announced, with no wisecracking in his voice, "Bandit, three o'clock!" And no sooner were the words out than Sergeant Rack shouted, "Main drive temperatures going up!"

Events were moving with the lightning-quick pace of modern electronic warfare. Johnny Draxton automatically put the big spacecraft into a diving turn, reaching with his free hand for the tailpipe cooler nozzle control. He cut the starboard engines and laid on full thrust to the port mills, at the same time kicking the near impulse retainer gear control with his foot. For a moment it looked as though this unorthodox and daring maneuver would succeed; but then a tight pattern of laser impulses ripped through the pilot's compartment. The ship's skin sealed over at once. But Johnny cursed, grinned tightly, and slumped forward. A trickle of blood seeped from under his crushed flight cap.

The big ship nosed over more steeply, screaming down toward the grinning dragon on Mnos II.

Young Deverell's gray eyes met the sergeant's blue ones and clung for a moment. The young pilot could see that the old sergeant's face, usually the color of a well-ridden Baluchistani saddle, had bleached to a shade approximating kidskin.

Deverell considered this as the ship plummeted downward. He thought of his gray-haired soldier-father, his fiancée, the Space Academy, the flag, the anthem, and San Francisco, which he had never seen. Then, with icy steadiness, he reached out and gripped the twin throttles, the rudder, the stick, and the side-thrust retaining gear

Can You Feel Anything When I Do This? 159

control, and eased them all back with a single powerful pull from his shoulders.

In the rear of the ship, an announcement came over the intercom: "Crew, man your battle stations." For a moment no one recognized the icy, purposeful voice. Then Ash said, "Gawd, it's the lieutenant!"

No one laughed. St. Augustus Lee, his family and heritage forgotten, picked up a crescent wrench and moved to the blockback flasher assembly. Bombardier Bluefeather, his bronze face impassive, rolled back the twin interlocks on his bombsight and peered through the delicate instrument with eyes that for centuries had scanned the rolling hills of the Sioux Nation. Ash, no wisecrack on his lips, set his battery of computer-operated laser guns to automatic tracking. And Sergeant Rack, with no time now to think of coffee or generals, no time even to think of his wife Myra who was not allowed in the Service Canteen because she was Indonesian, moved quietly to his task of preparing the enormous spaceship for self-destruction in case the impossible should occur.

The Kalnakak bandit ship suddenly sheered off. They could see the yellowish glow of his warp-reactors as he streaked away into deep space. That was just like the Kalnakak—to bluff to the limit of Terran endurance, then back off and wait for a better opportunity! And still the big spaceship, her outer skin now glowing white-hot, screamed toward the surface of Mnos II.

"Shall I jettison, sir?" asked Sergeant Rack.

"Not a chance!" roared young Deverell. "We're not going to lose one scrap of Terran equipment! I'm going to power her out of here!"

"But, sir!" the sergeant cried, "you'll tear the engines right off her!"

"Then let them come off," Deverell gritted, and his big, clumsy-looking but amazingly deft hands closed hard on the controls.

Johnny Draxton, just coming back to consciousness,

looked up; but no expression crossed his face. Quietly he lighted a cigar.

And the instrument panel glittered like a Christmas tree gone berserk!

Mach forces rose with dizzying speed. There was a moment of utter horror when they heard the ominous sound of something breaking away; but it was only young Deverell, ripping away his jacket so he could breathe better.

Slowly, unwillingly, the ship took the cruel stress and pulled out of the dive. By the time they were fully out of it, the ship was half a light-year beyond Mnos II, streaking toward the Lesser Magellanic Cloud. But they were safe, and their multi-billion dollar spacecraft was still in one piece.

Back aft, St. Augustus Lee let out a deep breath of air. He found that he didn't really care about the War between the States any longer. In fact, he could even think of it as the Civil War. After all, they *were* one country now. Bluefeather had the shadow of a grin on his taciturn face; he knew that the corn would be tall in the Apache country this year. And Gunner Ash, after shakily lighting a cigarette, said, "Man! How about that!"

This time they all laughed at the irrepressible Brooklyn boy's quip.

A little blood still oozed from under Johnny Draxton's crushed cap where the laser beam had creased him. He said, "Well, Lieutenant, you may be a general's son, but I think you'll do. Yessir, I think you'll just maybe do."

Lieutenant Deverell, looking very young yet somehow very old, said, "Captain, you are leaning against the nose-assembly release toggle. Good thing it's interlocked."

Captain Johnny Draxton, veteran of more than three hundred combat missions, tiger extraordinary, looked startled, then angry, then abashed. At last he grinned.

After a long moment, Deverell grinned, too.

The two men shook hands as the huge GP-1077F2 screamed silently through the near-vacuum of space.